A BRUSH WITH PASSION
A TRILOGY—BOOK ONE

VIENNA PATTERNS

A BRUSH WITH PASSION

A TRILOGY—BOOK ONE

VIENNA PATTERNS

A HISTORICAL NOVEL ABOUT
GUSTAV KLIMT AND EMILIE FLÖGE

JOAN KELLEY

A BRUSH WITH PASSION: A TRILOGY—
BOOK ONE—VIENNA PATTERNS
A HISTORICAL NOVEL ABOUT GUSTAV KLIMT AND EMILIE FLÖGE

iUniverse books may be ordered through booksellers or by contacting:

iUniverse
1663 Liberty Drive
Bloomington, IN 47403
www.iuniverse.com
1-800-Authors (1-800-288-4677)

ISBN: 978-1-5320-4830-2 (sc)
ISBN: 978-1-5320-4831-9 (e)

Library of Congress Control Number: 2018904901

Print information available on the last page.

iUniverse rev. date: 06/28/2018

Dedicated to my mentor and friend,
Professor Christian M. Nebehay,
his gracious wife Reneé Nebehay-King,
and my surrogate grandmother Dr. Vita Künstler.
These wonderful people are still alive in spirit.

PREFACE

In September 1986, I attended a multi-media production of *Vienna Lusthaus* at the Kennedy Center in Washington, D.C. My knowledge about *fin de siècle* Vienna was slight, but I knew the era was considered restless and passionate. To my surprise, I found the production disappointing, or to quote my daughter, "It was boring." I complained to a friend, "There was no exposed nerve. Nothing took my breath away." He replied, "What you felt was missing I think you'll find on the walls of the Museum of Modern Art in New York. Check out an exhibit called 'Vienna 1900'. Look for these two guys, Klimt and Schiele."

My turn to become restless and passionate: I went to New York City and scheduled a morning at MoMA where 'Vienna 1900' radiated from the walls in its final week. At the end of a corridor, Gustav Klimt's *The Kiss* glowed on a wall. I was stunned. Nearby, a life-sized photograph of Klimt in his garden, looking playful and earthy, holding a black and white kitten.

He looked at me and said, "You."

"Me *what?*"

Then I saw Klimt's *Portrait of Emilie Flöge*. According to the caption, Flöge had been Klimt's companion for 27 years. "Ahhh," I nodded, "that's what he wants me to do." I went to the museum shop and bought as many books, prints and posters as I could carry away. In that hour, my life changed.

I wrote to the author of the first book I read, art history professor Dr. Alessandra Comini, telling her I wanted to write a one-woman show about Emilie Flöge. She replied, "That's a noble project, but if you're serious, you should be in touch with [Klimt expert] Professor Christian Nebehay in Vienna. But be prepared for rejection—he's very busy." I wrote to Professor Nebehay; he responded by return mail.

The next three years included four intense research trips to Vienna, bursting with adventure, frustration and joy; countless hours with four German-speaking translators; building friendships with talented Austrian scholars, artists, actors and museum directors; embracing a computer as a new member of my family; reading at least 40 books three times each, absorbing more details with each reading; shooting thousands of color slides of Vienna and buying dozens of music tapes from the period (I am the first person to discover Gustav Mahler, of course.); framing more than 100 prints and posters for my walls; keeping voluminous notes on yellow legal-sized paper, and finally, in 1989, producing and directing a two-part, two-evening staged reading version of my historical novel, *Vienna Patterns*, at the renowned Vienna's English Theatre. The reading featured 14 actors and was enhanced by 300-plus slides, 60 brief musical interludes between scenes, costumes and lights.

I was no longer restless—just passionate. Because of Gustav Klimt, I've known more love than this world usually allows one person.

A great deal more has been written about Klimt and his circle since my plunge into existing 1986 literature. My imagined characters and scenes far outnumber accurate information, however. I hope my fantasies and the facts paint their own picture. Much of my information came from my mentor, Professor Nebehay, whose father, Gustav Nebehay, was Klimt's executor. At one point, I felt that the more I learned, the more I needed to know. Professor Nebehay told me, "You know as much as anyone. Just begin." So I did.

The original one-woman show grew almost immediately into a reading, then into the following novel. The second and third manuscripts, *Diamonds and Sand* and *Dirty Linen*, followed—"making themselves known to me"—during the next two decades.

As pretentious and preposterous as this may seem, I believe Gustav Klimt chose me. From the moment he stared at me from MoMA's wall, I felt claimed. I know I was waiting for him. Perhaps we were waiting for one another.

About Vienna Patterns

The curtain rises on Vienna in the late 19th Century. Monumental buildings line the gracious Ringstrasse, a wide boulevard that embraces the Inner City. The revered music of Brahms, Beethoven, Bach, Haydn, Mozart and Strauss bursts from elegant concert halls. The vast Stephansdom Cathedral towers majestically over the City's center. Beautifully attired women drop by Demel's for afternoon tea, flavored with gossip. Fabled Lipizzaner horses enchant audiences with their perfected routines. Prosperous men exchange financial rumors in richly appointed, smoky clubs. And the Danube, always the Danube, glides peacefully by, keeping Vienna's secrets....

But backstage, Vienna is changing its costume. Writers Hugo Von Hofmannsthal, Arthur Schnitzler, Karl Kraus, Felix Salten, and many others, explore life beneath the City's glossy surface. The music of Gustav Mahler and Arnold Schönberg soars in new directions, testing the ear and patience of conservative audiences. A dozen different nationalities crowd into narrow alleys beyond the Inner City, and confront Vienna's tinsel façade. The growing odor of anti-Semitism chokes the air.

Center stage is Gustav Klimt, Vienna's most famous and infamous artist. He abandons tradition, paints complex patterns and gives form to sexuality, labeled by some as pornographic. The man is as commanding as his work.

During this tempestuous scene, a talented designer, Emilie Flöge, opens an *haute couture* dress shop, the Schwestern Flöge – a highly unusual undertaking for a woman. The visionary Emilie creates flowing, comfortable, stunning gowns for Vienna's more adventuresome women. The gowns free women from miserable corsets, unhealthy, tortured tiny waists, and movement-inhibiting bustles.

Into Emilie Flöge's world strides irresistible Gustav Klimt. For the next 27 years, with Emilie by his side, Klimt knows criticism and censure, praise and fame. Their tempestuous relationship lasts until Klimt's death… and beyond.

Through *Vienna Patterns*, find yourself in a time that may never be equaled for fashion, fabulous art, and fascinating personalities: *fin de siècle* Vienna. The era is very theatrical. Very… Vienna….

.‾.

If you want to understand me, look at my paintings.
— *Gustav Klimt*

CONTENTS

PART TWO

PART ONE

Memories

Oh, God… I wish you could have seen this place. It was so… beautiful… filled with light and energy. Gustav used to sit on this window sill swinging his legs and making paper airplanes to shoot at the patrons below in the Casa Piccola's outdoor café on Mariahilferstrasse. He had very good aim.

There was a table right in the center of the room—and chairs. Not very comfortable chairs, actually. One had to behave in Josef Hoffmann's chairs. And lovely glass cabinets against this wall. Friederike Maria Beer hid cigars in these cabinets. She loved to smoke in front of the other customers. "It's no fun being naughty unless someone knows," she said, blowing filmy blue smoke rings.

And in front of a lovely mirror was a mannequin Gustav designed. He constructed a little—well, it was make of feathers and beads and fur and he pasted it ... here ... and no one knew because of course the mannequin kept her clothes on, in contrast to nearly all the other women in Gustav's life. That bit of feathers and fur was one of our many little secrets. Pleasant memories ... before any pain.…

I remember the first time I saw this room. Gustav brought me here. He led me up the staircase and at the top of the stairs, he covered my eyes with his hands, then released them with a flourish.

"Now!"

"What is it?"

"It's your new shop!"

"But it's awful! It's grim, it's dark!"

Then I heard footsteps on the stairs: Josef Hoffmann and Kolo Moser.

"It's wonderful! It's perfect!" Moser cried.

"That wall will have to come down," Hoffmann scowled.

"I love it!" Moser rejoiced. He rejoiced easily.

"The ceiling will have to be lowered," Hoffman growled. He growled often.

I leaned forward. "Wait a moment, don't I have a say in any of this?"

Hoffmann turned and squinted at me as though he were noticing me for the first time.

"No, my dear, you haven't," he said, apparently astonished that I would even voice an opinion.

Gustav laughed, folded his arms across his chest ... and that was my introduction to this wonderful space!

.‾.‾.‾.‾.‾.‾.‾.‾.‾.‾.‾.‾.‾.‾.‾.‾.‾.‾.‾.

Meeting Klimt

My name is Emilie Flöge. I was born in 1874 to Hermann and Barbara Flöge. My father made meerschaum pipes and exported them to England. My two older sisters and I did all the things expected of daughters in a middle class Viennese family: We took lessons. Drawing lessons, sewing lessons, piano lessons, French lessons, ballroom dancing lessons, and how to be charming lessons, with an emphasis on when to be quiet. Young ladies were advised to be quiet most of the time.

Helene and Pauline were better students in the art of quiet than I was. Quiet as a career did not interest me. My favorite activities were talking and drawing and dancing. At 17, waltzing was the closest thing to ecstasy I knew.

The waltz was free and mad and suspect! People waltzed all night. Special rooms were reserved near the ballroom for women "in a family way" (before it became obvious), or those who needed to loosen the laces in their corsets for a few moments, or else they'd faint.

In my bedroom, I often danced until I was delirious. I was only allowed to attend dances with my parents and sisters, of course. This brings us to Fasching and the Opera Ball. But tonight, the very night of this most gorgeous of all balls, my parents are engaged at the last moment with some of Father's business associates from England. We begged Father to let us attend with our brother Hermann, as chaperone.

"We promise not to take our gloves off," Helene said with great sincerity.

"We shall, of course, return by a decent hour," Pauline promised earnestly.

"And we'll not dance more than twice in succession so no one will see us perspiring," I added, trying to appear both sincere and earnest.

Father looked from one anxious face… to the other…to the other. "I will grant permission only providing your brother never lets you out of his sight."

Hermann adopted his trustworthy expression, perfected in front of the bathroom mirror while waiting for his moustache to grow. "I shall even force myself to dance with them. With pleasure, of course."

Father stared at us a moment for effect. "I'm sure I needn't remind you to comport yourselves graciously and modestly at all times." We squealed with joy, kissed Father noisily and tore upstairs to dress.

Dressing was not a casual event, it took hours. While we dressed, we gossiped. Our most delicious gossip concerned Helene and Ernst Klimt, Gustav Klimt's younger brother.

The Klimt brothers were in their 20s and already widely respected as fine decorative painters. With Franz Matsch, their childhood friend, they'd won impressive commissions to paint murals in public buildings, and create elaborate illustrations on theatre curtains. They spent months on scaffolds, which Ernst Klimt said was unbearable. And everything had to have a historical basis, which Gustav Klimt said—well, Helene said he used a bad word, but she wouldn't tell me what it was.

Gustav Klimt received the *Kaiserpreis* for painting the audience as seen from the stage in the old Burgtheater before it was torn down. Imagine, more than 100 people were recognizable in the painting. And it's a small painting!

One of them was the Emperor Franz Joseph's mistress, actress Katarina Schratt. Mother thought her presence in the painting "distasteful." Hmm. As far as I could tell, it was all right for the Emperor to *have* a mistress, but it was not all right for Katarina Schratt to *be* a mistress. Confusing. The entire subject of men and women was a mystery to me, and I suspected that everyone in the world knew more about it than I did.

My efforts to discover life's secrets pertaining to this subject had been thus far very unsatisfactory. Two years ago, as Mother and I were stuffing chickens at the kitchen counter, I asked, almost as casually as I'd rehearsed the question, "Is there something I should know about *men?*"

"Just study your Father, dear," Mother said, waving the salt shaker vaguely. "He's an excellent example of a man."

"No, I mean about men and *women*."

"Oh. I think we could use more bread crumbs. Emilie, just study the chickens, then."

So every time I saw a chicken, I scrutinized its every move, but I did not learn its secrets. What I learned was how to walk like a chicken. One Sunday, Helene watched me from the back porch as I picked my way around the yard. "Emilie, what on earth are you doing?"

"I'm a chicken."

"No, you're an embarrassment."

I hate secrets.

Intuition tells me that Gustav Klimt knows everything I'm curious about, and surely much I couldn't imagine. He has a dreadful reputation, and Father told Helene that she must never be alone with him. He also told Ernst this, and poor Ernst blushed, Helene reported.

Helene is 20 and she has never been in love before. "What does it feel like?" I asked her as I tortured her hair into fat curls.

"It's hard to describe."

"But how will I know if it ever happens to me?"

"Oh, you'll know, Emilie, believe me, you'll know." I did not consider this a very useful answer. "Emilie, be careful, you're pulling my hair!"

The ball was glorious! The chandeliers sparkled and trembled as the dancers swept across the polished floor. Hermann brought me a glass of champagne as a bribe for not telling our parents that he danced three times with Alma Schindler. All the young men in Vienna fancied themselves in love with Alma. Or so she supposed.

Last summer, Alma and I were in the same outdoor painting class in the Prater. One afternoon, she stood rudely close to my shoulder, watching me work. "I understand you *sew* really well," she said, blinking her blank blue eyes. I turned to her and smiled, "I do. It's a shame you're unable to find a good dressmaker." She gasped and stomped back to her easel. Stomping loses its effect on grass.

I was swaying to the music, sipping my champagne and feeling aglow, when I saw him across the ballroom, and my cheeks flamed, and my clothes burned away, and my entire body… well—

I don't know if I moved toward him, or if he moved toward me, but suddenly, he was standing before me with eyes that knew all my secrets! (Actually, I didn't have any yet.) Without even introducing himself, he said, very slowly, "I think we need to know one another."

No one had ever said anything like that to me before. Then I heard myself saying, "Would you like to dance, Herr Klimt?" I asked *him!*

"No. But I would like to take a walk with you. I will ask Ernst to arrange it." His eyes blazed, and his aura lit the entire room. And then two bright, bold women slipped their arms through his and drew him away.

I rushed from the ballroom and leaned against a marble pillar at the top of the grand staircase. I thought I might faint. And I'm *not* the fainting type. Pauline rustled to my side, clutching her skirts tightly. "I saw you talking with Gustav Klimt. What did he say? What did he do?" Pauline looked horrified. That relaxed me.

"I think he changed my life."

"But you just met him. Surely that's not possible."

"Yes, I'm afraid it is," I said matter-of-factly, as though I made such pronouncements every day. Suddenly, I thought about chickens. Mother lied.

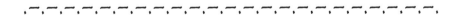

The Meeting

On Sundays, everyone who counted drove their carriages around the Ringstrasse. Being seen in elegant carriages drawn by

smart horses was *de rigueur*. (Because I took French for two years, I can use words like *de rigueur*.) The women wore huge hats and their skirts were so full there was barely room in the carriage for their male escorts. As the carriages passed one another, everyone nodded, and the men tipped their silk hats, and it was all very boring. I hate being bored.

Walking was more fun, I thought. Father saw no reason to walk when we could be driven. "The Klimts walk because they have to. The Flöges ride because they can," he reasoned.

Gustav and Ernst Klimt's father was a goldsmith from Bohemia, and came from a different class than ours. That's why Father was hesitant about Ernst, initially. But Ernst was intelligent and talented, and so clearly devoted to Helene that Father was won over. He consented to their courtship because they followed his rules: They saw one another no oftener than twice a week and usually within the confines of our family. Ernst was already established as one of Vienna's outstanding painters—second only to Gustav, I thought. The Klimt brothers, and their friend Franz Matsch, banded together to form The Artists' Company, as they called themselves.

All Vienna agreed that the mantle of Painter Prince was to have passed from Hans Makart to Gustav Klimt. When I was very young, Father and I visited Makart's atelier to deliver a meerschaum pipe. I was fascinated with the huge room: In addition to enormous paintings of over-fed, tumbling women, the room was stuffed with grinning bears' heads, dusty draperies, and vases overflowing with brittle dried grass… and obviously, no peacock was safe when Makart was around.

Father found Makart's atelier "unreasonably grandiose. Such ostentation leads to confusion," he announced. Father was a firm believer in order and moderation. He approved of the fact that Ernst was saving money so that he might properly provide for

Helene. By contrast, Gustav felt that, "money should circulate," and so never had any, Ernst told Helene.

Makart died while he was young and still handsome. He masterminded a huge parade with a hundred floats, and as much pomp and circumstance as Vienna has ever seen. The event was in celebration of the Emperor and Empress's 25th wedding anniversary. Some people said Makart worked himself to death. Others whispered he died of something no one would talk about. Anyway, he died.

We expected Ernst to propose to Helene any day, although Father had hoped Pauline would marry first, since she was the oldest. But she was already 24, and had no beaux. "I enjoy my piano more than I do men, truth be known. All one is expected to do to a piano is dust it and keep it tuned. Men require constant upkeep."

I was told every other week that if I expected to attract a refined and suitable husband, I must keep my opinions to myself. "You would vex the patience of Job himself," Father was fond of saying.

Well, on the appointed Sunday, Father decided that Pauline should join us for the walk, otherwise she would be left at home alone because our cook and maid were allowed Sunday off. A message was sent to Ernst, who then invited his older sister, Klara. "Why not invite the entire *city?*" I wailed. To myself.

So five Flöges were joined by three Klimts and off we marched. Gustav is a powerful man—broad shouldered, with a dark complexion. I sensed he could walk farther and faster than any of us.

"He looks like a butcher," Mother whispered to me. And although the entire gathering was secretly engineered so that Gustav and I could be together, he spent most of the walk telling Father about his latest commission, and being very polite, and putting everyone at ease.

After an hour, Mother confided, "Well, if he *were* a butcher, I think I could rely on him to provide us with a very nice cut of meat." I recognized this as high recommendation, of a sort.

The day was lovely—a spring sun warmed our foreheads and lifted our hearts. I was so aware of Gustav Klimt's presence that I hardly looked at him for fear he would recognize my admiration.

Then, just before our two families parted, he fell in step with me. "My judgment tells me that this has been a very successful outing," he said softly. I glanced sideways at the brown face. He was looking at me, and his eyes were happy.

"I expect in many things you have good judgment, Herr Klimt," I said carefully.

"Often enough, thus far. We have now made a beginning, Fraulein Emilie Flöge." And he touched his index finger to his lips and strode off to join Ernst and Klara.

As soon as the Klimts left, Helene rushed up to me. "What did he say?"

"He said, 'Ernst is not only a wonderful painter, he is a very fortunate man,'" I replied in a moment of genius.

"You know, Gustav Klimt is a much nicer man than I thought he would be," Helene said, beaming.

The Kitchen

So now you know the "good beginning". Of course, I thought I would hear from Gustav Klimt immediately—that evening, the next morning, surely by the next week. "He's terribly busy, he's in great demand," Helene explained over and over. "Besides, he's much too old for you. And Father would never approve." Naturally, I did not hear a word she said.

I didn't know much about Gustav Klimt, except that he was beautiful. I could sense him at will: I could see him, hear him, touch him, smell him. Everything else in life became gauzy, slightly unreal. My fantasies were real. They focused on conversations. We sat, side by side, and talked for hours. With him, I was bright, funny, brave—and, I imagined, more appealing than any other woman in his life.

All Vienna knew, or thought they knew, scandalous stories about Gustav Klimt. But I was protected and naive and besides, no one could have convinced me that he was not whatever I wanted him to be.

My feelings confused me greatly. Intense, heavens, *yes*, intense. I felt on the verge of a fatal illness at all times! Helene found my ardor "amusing and adorable." Pauline found it "inappropriate at first glance and deranged if one really thinks about it." Older sisters are not one of life's necessities.

When Ernst visited Helene, they were allowed to sit in the front parlor, which was filled with Biedermeier furniture, and proper paintings in huge frames, and our piano. The room looked fat.

Ernst and Helene's major activity was whispering. Helene also giggled, musically, and they discussed their future *ad nauseam*. I interrupted as often as possible. Would they mind if I practiced my Mozart? Would they like more coffee or torte? I needed to look at Ernst. He resembled Gustav minus the smolder. His eyes did not burn, and his body knew how to relax. Gustav's energy kept his body, well, ready. I had no idea what I meant by that.

But my fantasies wore a bit thin. I had not seen Gustav Klimt in three months. In the meantime, Ernst asked for Helene's hand in marriage. "I hope he's willing to take the rest of you, too," I teased.

"Emilie," Mother said, "That remark was inappropriate." People *loved* that word!

The wedding preparations were sumptuous. For my part, I begged to design the gowns, which I decided should be unique: They should be comfortable.

"Comfortable?" exclaimed Helene.

"Yes, comfortable."

"But no one considers comfort. That's what nightgowns are for. I want to be fashionable."

"And miserable."

"Well, misery is an unfortunate but necessary part of being fashionable."

"Why? Why can't a woman experience the joy of wearing clothing that allows her to move, to delight in how her body feels? I hate corsets, and wearing dead whales around my waist!"

"Emilie, you are so strange. How did you come to be so strange?" Helene sighed.

"Helene, let's make a bargain. I'll design a wedding gown for you, and gowns for Mother and Pauline and me, and if you don't like them, hire whoever you like to make you a miserable gown, and I'll wear whatever you decide, and I just won't breathe, and I'll probably die, but that's all right, that can be part of the bargain."

"Emilie, how did you come to be so different?"

"I don't know." And I didn't.

Well, Mother gave me permission to design the gowns. I drew beautiful, floating, ethereal dresses, and I liked them! They would shimmer, they would exult our bodies and our souls. I kept the drawings a secret. I wanted them to be exactly right before I had to defend them to Helene and Mother. I worked on them after school, often on the kitchen table where the afternoon light was best.

Late one afternoon, as I was agonizing over a detail on Helene's gown, our maid, Gerti, came into the kitchen.

"Herr Klimt is here."

I thought, "Oh, Ernst is here early."

"Ask him to join me in the kitchen," I told Gerti, and was about to hide my drawings from Ernst when Gustav Klimt strode into the kitchen!

"Ernst is ill. He wanted Helene to know he won't be taking her to the Volkstheater tonight. I volunteered to deliver the message. I had hoped to find you just as you are, Fraulein Emilie."

"How is that?" was all I could think to say.

"Flushed. Unguarded. Quite lovely."

"You are, of course, most welcome in our home, Herr Klimt. I'll find Mother and tell her we have a guest. Oh, no, I'm afraid she's gone to tea. Somewhere."

"Emilie?"

"Yes?"

"Gently."

My panic dissolved, a little, and we smiled at one another while Gerti, tight-lipped and suspicious, gravely stood guard.

"Gerti, some coffee and pastries for Herr Klimt," I said, trying to sound like Mother.

"I will trade you a strudel for a consultant's fee," he said, nodding at my smudged drawings. And for the next hour, we hunched over my designs and argued and laughed and finally agreed. And by the end of the coffee and the collaboration, we had four of the most marvelous gowns Vienna would ever see. And he loved my idea that women should not have to suffer to look beautiful.

"Women should wear only black stockings," he mumbled to himself.

"With everything?

"No, I mean they should wear nothing except stockings, preferably black and weather permitting. My child, you are blushing, forgive me. Now. We have had a good walk and a good talk. What do you think should be next? He leaned back in the kitchen chair and looked at me the way no one else has, ever.

"I think… next… we should rejoice in the marriage of your brother to my sister." Everything in me wanted to say something wild but I couldn't!

Klimt reached across the space between us and touched my temple with his thumb. He drew a line from my eyebrow diagonally down to the corner of my mouth. The nerves in my face tingled. "You are quite right," he said, and the smile was kind and patient and amused.

Gerti appeared, wiping her hands on her apron. "Could you possibly have been responsible for that strudel?" Klimt asked her. Gerti nodded, apprehensively. "My Mother's strudel now has an equal. I will not tell my Mother." Gerti almost smirked as she showed Klimt to the door.

I rushed to my room, and from the window, watched Klimt stride into the purple dusk. I felt like stained glass: Breakable and exquisite. I retraced his touch on my cheek. Oh God, oh God….

.⌐.⌐.⌐.⌐.⌐.⌐.⌐.⌐.⌐.⌐.⌐.⌐.⌐.⌐.⌐.⌐.⌐.⌐.

The Wedding

This was the World's First Wedding. It's all we talked about. The Turkish sieges (either one of them), the Corpus Christi Processions, Emperor Franz Joseph's Silver Anniversary Jubilee— all were casual events compared with this wedding.

Helene changed her mind about everything at least six times. *Except* her wedding gown. We all agreed the drawing was perfect. Mother hired two seamstresses for our gowns, but I was committed to making Helene's gown myself. Using another pattern, I adapted it and cut a new pattern, basted it, fitted her, sewed it, fitted her, did the finish work, fitted her.

"No bride has ever spent so much time in her gown before her wedding," Helene laughed. I think everyone was worried: Could I make the dress look like the drawing? My first miracle. I did.

There were many parties, gifts arrived daily, and Helene and Ernst spent as much time alone as they could manage. (Our cellar landing became as popular as the Cafe Central.) On the afternoon before the wedding day, the Klimts invited our family and close friends to a *heurige* for music and wine. Father did not look forward to the event.

"Those places are so *lower class*," he grumbled.

"Hermann, don't you dare let Helene hear you," Mother scolded.

At this time, Gustav was painting 11 spandrals and intercolumnal panels at the Kunsthistorisches Museum in Italian and Egyptian and Greek styles. The one I liked best looked like a red-haired cleaning girl named Frieda whom Mother let go about a year ago. Not my idea of a Greek goddess, more a Viennese girl of "easy virtue", as Mother called them, her voice full of Meaning.

Anyway, Gustav was there with his sisters Klara, Hermine, and Johanna, and of course with brothers Georg and Ernst. The violin and accordion players knew folk songs from the provinces, and we sat under a grape arbor at wooden tables, and sang heartily, especially Frau Anna Klimt.

"Your mother has a wonderful voice, Ernst," I said.

"She wanted to be an opera singer. But she married my father instead," he told me. For the first time, I wondered: Could a woman, possibly, do both?

Father could not bring himself to sit at the same table as Ernst's Father at first, but as the late afternoon warmth began to melt inhibitions, even Father had a hard time remaining aloof. In spite of himself, I could tell Father was beginning to like Ernst's parents, and it did not hurt that Ernst most certainly would enjoy a brilliant future.

After enough wine, Father became almost expansive. The two fathers smoked cigars and Father praised Ernst and Herr Klimt praised Helene.

I was giddy with the feel of fading sunlight, the fragrance of wine, and the sound of sentimental music and laughter. Then Ernst asked Helene to dance, and Gustav asked me!

He didn't exactly ask. He stood before me, extended his hands, and said, "You asked me once if I wanted to dance with you. I said no. But I do now."

Very formally, I placed my hands in his and he drew me to my feet. Slowly, he encircled my waist and then swooped me into the music. Madly, we swirled between the tables! Sweat gleamed on his forehead, and he smelled earthy and—well, I didn't have a name for it yet. My eyes never left his, and I felt we could do no wrong. I had never been so happy in my life! I was dizzy with new wine, with the explosions of sun through the grape leaves above, with the strange thrill of being held by this man. Somewhere in the daze, I thought, "Helene, you were right. *This* is what love feels like!"

I remember that moment better than I do the wedding. Everything moved so fast. I wanted to cry, "Stop! Let's do this again, so we can hold onto it!" We do that all our lives, don't we?

The Klimt/Flöge gowns were a great success, and Helene and Ernst were the sweetest, most adoring couple in the world. "One is almost embarrassed in their presence," Pauline said, fanning herself, and watching our sister and her handsome groom nuzzling each other, and glowing with anticipation.

"I hope this moment lasts for them forever," I said.

"Why, Emilie, dear, you're crying." Pauline put her arm around my shoulders.

1892

New Year's Eve. *Prost!* At the beginning of the year, the Klimt brothers and Matsch were painting scenes from famous theaters of the past on the new Burgtheater staircases and ceilings, and they needed models. Well, who better than the Klimt and Flöge families? There certainly were enough of us. Even Matsch modeled a Renaissance costume, and he looked splendid in tights.

"I love to look at men's legs," I told Pauline.

"You're not supposed to, that's indecent!"

"Then why did those Renaissance men wear tights? That doesn't make sense."

"Emilie, there are many things one thinks but mustn't say," Pauline replied, looking flustered. Hmm.

I was thrilled that Gustav asked me to model, but I wasn't very good at it. I was nervous, and couldn't hold still. Finally, he said, "Don't look at me. Look at the point where the wall and ceiling meet in the corner, and tell someone in your head all the things you don't dare say aloud."

"Well! I think I love you, Gustav Klimt, and I don't care what everyone says about you, you are kind and gentle and you make me feel as though my bone marrow has turned to chicken fat and I know that's not very romantic but it's true and I wish you would…" And here my monologue drifted into feelings I couldn't give words to yet.

When the painting was completed, we invited the Klimts to a party at our house. Gerti made another perfect strudel and Father and Herr Klimt played horseshoes, and Father passed out his *good* cigars.

Pauline played the piano, and Frau Klimt sang in her strong contralto. But the *piece de resistance* of the evening was Ernst's announcement that he and Helene were going to become parents. This meant Gustav would be the baby's uncle and I would be its aunt. That was almost incestuous—another word I didn't know yet.

I think Gustav was the happiest member of the family. He hugged Ernst and kissed Helene on both cheeks and hugged Ernst again. We toasted the radiant couple. Helene smiled shyly and clung to Ernst's arm, while Ernst looked "proud as a peacock," to quote Mother. Gustav touched his glass to mine and said quietly, "To birth." I fell asleep with that phrase in my head.

On the eve of Gustav's 30th birthday, his father died of a massive stroke. Anna Klimt was devastated. She'd lost a daughter when the child was five and sometimes talked to herself. Now she just sat by the coffin, mumbling. I'm not sure Gustav even recognized me at the funeral. I touched his sleeve and said, "I'm truly sorry." He just nodded.

I decided the only thing I could do to help, even a little, was to make a lovely dress for Helene to wear when she needed more room in her clothes. "Let's give the baby space to breathe," I told Helene. "We'll give you an Empire waistline and you'll be beautiful. Everyone will want to look like you."

Helene kissed me. "The baby thanks you, Emilie."

In November, Ernst was one of the artists asked to greet Emperor Franz Joseph at the opening of Anselm Feurbach's exhibit in the Great Hall of the Academy of Fine Arts. The weather was bitterly cold and Ernst only wore his morning-coat. He waited on the steps of the Academy for half-an-hour before the Emperor arrived.

The next day, Ernst awoke with a fever. The doctor told Helene it was influenza. He assured her that Ernst would be up and about in a week. He wasn't. He developed a terrible cough and Helene and Frau Klimt administered mustard plasters, and put herbs in hot water for him to breathe, and boiled brown sugar and onions and turpentine for him to swallow.

He felt well enough to come to the table for soup on the evening of 9 December, wrapped in blankets and trembling. Helene fed him a bowl of steaming broth and they talked about the baby.

"If it's a boy, I'd like to name him after my father," he whispered. "And if it's a girl, let's name her Helene. My first Helene is nearly perfect, surely my second would—" Then he coughed blood and fell onto the table, spilling the broth.

Later that night, at age 28, Ernst Klimt died.

.⎺.⎺.⎺.⎺.⎺.⎺.⎺.⎺.⎺.⎺.⎺.⎺.⎺.⎺.⎺.⎺.⎺.

The Funeral

Someone said the Viennese are like a two-room apartment: One room is bright, sunny, attractive, calm. The other room is dark, gloomy, barren, mysterious. Extremes and ambivalence are woven into the fabric of Viennese life. I didn't know that then, but later this truth became clear to me.

Even when I was 17, I fought Vienna's darker moods. I was afraid of extremes, but the Viennese certainly embraced them. The suicide rate in Vienna was higher than anywhere else in the world. I had always considered suicide an over-reaction to a bad day. But when Ernst died, I smelled its breath. *Nothing was dependable* anymore! I felt as though I were standing on a slippery rock in a raging river.

We tried not to leave Helene alone. But one evening, as I walked past the guest bedroom where she had been staying since Ernst's death, I heard her sobbing, "I want to die, I want to die!" I opened the door and found her sitting on the floor next to the bed. I was frightened, but I knelt beside her, stroked her hair, and felt inexpressible fury at the obscenity of Ernst's death. *"No you don't! Life is even more precious now,"* I said, rocking her.

She took my hand and placed it on her round stomach. "The baby's kicking, Emilie." This was the first time I'd seen her smile since Ernst died.

The shock of Ernst's death sobered all of Vienna. We Viennese celebrate death with more macabre enthusiasm than almost any other event. We even have a funeral museum. Mother and Father constantly visited dead people. They counted funeral wreaths to determine who was the most popular among their recently departed friends and associates. But for the Klimt and Flöge families, the sorrow of Ernst's death—the *timing* of his death—would always remind us of the power of random tragedy.

Gustav delivered the eulogy, standing in the harsh December cold, snowflakes casually wandering onto his crimson face:

"This man—a son, a brother, a friend, a husband, a father, an artist—leaves his creative gifts, his nobility, and his uniqueness to each of us. No one will ever replace him. He will be a shining presence in my heart forever. I expect I speak for all of you: I love you, Ernst. Now. Always."

I did the only thing I could think of: I made another dress. Again, for Helene. This time, in black.

.⌐.⌐.⌐.⌐.⌐.⌐.⌐.⌐.⌐.⌐.⌐.⌐.⌐.⌐.⌐.⌐.⌐.⌐.

The Birth

Helene went into labor in the morning. By mid-afternoon, Mother sent for Frau Klimt and Doctor Zuckerkandl. There was much coming and going from the guest bedroom where Helene had stayed since Ernst's death three months ago.

I was terrified. "What if something happens?"

Pauline was incensed. "There must be a more logical way to give birth than this. I consider it bad planning on *Someone's* part." She had learned the Art of Emphasis from Mother.

We sat at the kitchen table, always the most comforting place in the house. Pauline knit baby booties and I embroidered—God knows what—on a pillowcase. I focused on the dull ticking of the Swiss tall clock in the hall because I didn't want to hear the doors and footsteps and the… noises upstairs.

Suddenly, Gustav Klimt burst into the kitchen, his hair wildly disheveled. He looked at me.

"Not yet."

"How long?"

"Since this morning."

He made a sound in his throat, strode from the room and bounded up the stairs.

"What on earth is that man doing?" Pauline demanded, slamming her knitting on the table. "Surely Father will stop him from entering the room!" Father was guarding the bedroom door as though gypsies were going to kidnap his new grandchild the moment it was born.

Pauline and I crept to the bottom of the stairs, holding hands, our hearts pounding. I heard the doctor's voice as well as Father's and Klimt's. Then the door closed and Pauline and I sat on the stairs, thinking of everything and nothing. I thought about dust. About how there was so much of it because of *all the furniture and vases and lamps with fringe and shawls and dried flowers and little marble statues and pillows and rugs on top of rugs and what was going on upstairs?*

And then, a tiny, frail cry. Pauline and I tore up the stairs. Father was white as a dumpling and his mouth trembled. He opened his arms and we rushed in. "Yes, indeed, thank God," he said into my hair.

Gustav Klimt opened the bedroom door. He was sweating, his sleeves were rolled to his elbows and his hands were red with blood. He looked triumphant.

"Your house has been blessed," he told Father. "Come."

We tiptoed into the room. Helene looked exhausted and awful and radiant all at the same time. Mother was bathing the child. "It's a girl," Helene said, as though this were the final right answer on a very important test.

Mother was cooing and the baby was bright scarlet and ugly, which worried me, but Mother said, "She is beautiful, just beautiful, my dear." Helene looked up at Gustav and held out her hand. She raised her eyebrows.

"Yes, he knows," Klimt said, taking her pale fingers in his.

"Immediately please, out," someone said, and we kissed Helene, who now held the tiny furious-looking creature with the squinched-up face.

Downstairs, Gerti warmed the goulash and Father sent Rudi, our man servant, to the cellar for wine. Klimt said to Father, "I cannot contain my joy. I need to walk. May I please have the pleasure of Fraulein Emilie's company on this wonderful night?"

"You are a good friend of the family, Herr Klimt. Don't be long."

Klimt's eyes at that moment, as he looked at me, were so full of everything that life does to us. I hope I don't need to tell you, I hope you've known the feeling. Wait, wait, I'm the one who's afraid of extremes, aren't I? At that age, I thought the ecstasy would outweigh the agony. But you never know. That's the glory and terror of life, isn't it?

Without a word, I walked beside Gustav Klimt to his atelier at Josefstädterstrasse 21. I had never been there before. It was a low villa with a garden left to grow wild. Even at dusk, I could sense the high protective trees, the flowers and creepers leading to the door.

Inside, gas street lights stretched fingers through the windows. The floors were covered with drawings—hundreds of them—on cheap brown wrapping paper. I felt as though I were in a sacred place.

Klimt took my hand and led me into a third studio. He struck a match, and lit candles. "Take off your coat." He stood without moving, concentrating on the flame. "I see women's bodies every day with my eyes. I want to see your body with my fingertips. I want to celebrate you. Ernst celebrated Helene. We are all blessed because of it."

And then Gustav Klimt looked at me. By the candlelight, I saw tiny lines forking toward his temple, tiny gold flecks in his beard. At that moment, I pledged myself hopelessly, without thought,
>   to the end of my childhood
>   to the veins beating in his temples
>   to the unborn children in his eyes
>   to the blood on his gentle hands
>   to the points of light circling his head
He knelt before me.
>   I was made oh oh oh
>   to be happy with you
>   forever

.⌐.⌐.⌐.⌐.⌐.⌐.⌐.⌐.⌐.⌐.⌐.⌐.⌐.⌐.⌐.⌐.⌐.

Vienna

Imagine a City of grand and imposing buildings, of gracious parks, spacious boulevards and handsome, proud people. Imagine a City bursting with art, music, scientific, and scholarly investigation. This was my City, my wonderful Vienna.

Vienna looked both East and West, in a country which had been ruled by one family for 600 years. Vienna was the coffeehouse where the brightest and most contentious wits gathered daily to argue and complain. Vienna was the enchanting forest running along the spine of the City, horseshoe-shaped green fields embracing the City on three sides. And the Danube, always the Danube, flowing passively from one century into the next.

A writer called Vienna "a gay, carefree City, reveling in the colorful and yeasty diversity that befits the capital of a huge multinational empire stretching from the Swiss to the Russian borders." As far as I knew, Vienna was the center of the universe.

Certainly no one could quarrel that it was the music center of Europe, anyway. Gluck, Salieri, Liszt, Brahms, Schubert, Mozart, Wagner, Haydn, the Strausses, and of course Beethoven; they all played or composed, lived or died in Vienna.

But perhaps the one person who most conspicuously epitomized Vienna was our Emperor, Franz Joseph. Whatever one thought about him, one had to admire his stamina. He came to the throne in 1848 at age 18. From then on, he read no book but the Army Register. When he was told about Krafft-Ebing's *Psychopathia Sexualis* in 1875, he said, "It's about time someone wrote a new Latin grammar."

From a distance, he worshipped his restless and vain wife, the Empress Elisabeth. To keep her freedom, Elisabeth protected his relationship with actress Katarina Schratt, in one of those strange royal arrangements the Viennese relished.

The Emperor's self-discipline was legendary. He slept on a narrow iron Army cot, bathed in a portable wooden tub, did not allow electric lights or indoor plumbing in the palace. I must confess: I am devoted to indoor plumbing.

He appeared all over Vienna, always smartly turned out in one of his 200 military uniforms. He attended concerts—and slept through most of them. He attended weddings—despite his own unhappy marriage. He smoked cheap government-issue cheroots and allowed himself only one glass of champagne a day. He was bound to ritual. When he was gravely ill and his doctor was called to his bedside at three in the morning, Franz Joseph rasped, "The dress!" and the doctor was hustled off to don his morning coat.

This sense of ritual held the Emperor together. He said, "The worst that can happen to a man in his lifetime has happened to me."

His brother, Maximillian, was executed by Mexican nationalists. His only son Rudolf committed suicide after shooting his 17-year-old mistress. He chose the royal hunting lodge at Mayerling for their fatal rendezvous. It was called the scandal of the century. (Father noted, "It creates a very bad example," and no one could argue with that!) The Empress Elisabeth was assassinated, and much later, so were the royal nephew—mean-spirited Franz Ferdinand and his wife, Sophia. Poor man, every time the Emperor turned around, *poof!* There went another member of the Imperial family.

Balancing an empire with 11 nationalities, and at least as many languages, took constant compromise. But Franz Joseph gave the illusion of continuity, of permanence. And indeed, when he came to the throne, nothing much had changed in the Dual Monarchy since medieval times, which was fine with Father: "I am certainly not against change, I just see no need for it," he maintained. "It gives one a sense of security at age 20 to know exactly what one will to be doing at age 50."

But one of Gustav's friends shook his head furiously, "That kind of security is death," he moaned.

"Bahr is a professional grumbler," Klimt explained, smiling.

"Klimt, you know perfectly well that nothing happens here, absolutely nothing." Hermann Bahr was called "The Man From The Day After Tomorrow." Nothing was ever *au courant* enough for him. "Someday, Fraulein, Herr Klimt and I will acquaint you with the other Vienna, the Vienna of impoverished bricklayers, of beds rented by the hour. When you are older."

Could it be that Vienna isn't really perfect after all? I wonder if Father knows this?

.⌐.⌐.⌐.⌐.⌐.⌐.⌐.⌐.⌐.⌐.⌐.⌐.⌐.⌐.⌐.⌐.⌐.⌐.⌐.

Assumptions

Fortunately, Father liked modern conveniences. It was social change that he objected to, and since we were quite comfortable, status quo made perfect sense to Father. "A place for everyone and everyone in his place," was one of his sayings. But anything science could do for him, he endorsed.

For example, he had nothing against a new contrivance called the telephone. He had one installed at his office, and another at home. He called Mother every afternoon to say, "I'm leaving the office now, my dear. Expect me in half an hour." This amused us because Father always left the office at the same time, and was always home in half an hour.

Of course, since few families owned telephones, there weren't many people to call. But Marie Breunig's family had a telephone and we talked daily. Marie was my best friend from finishing school. She always knew wonderful gossip.

"What can you two find to talk about every day?" Father chuckled.

"I'm telling Marie how Gustav Klimt knew me in the carnal fashion the night Heli was born, and how I've been longing for him to do it again, anytime, anywhere."

I didn't really say that. Here's what I do have to say, however: Never assume.

The night Gustav and I were intimate—I think that's what proper people call it—I assumed that we were, from that point on, a couple, that we would continue where Ernst and Helene were forced to stop. What could be more natural? Gustav was godfather to baby Heli and I was her godmother, so she was almost our child from the moment she was born.

My memory relived our "intimate" night over and over:

Klimt laid me on the bed in his atelier where the models pose. I am enveloped by the music of our sounds, the flushed planes of his "butcher's" brow, his tears spraying my face, mingling with my own. I feel—and welcome—exquisite pain, and finally, burning thanksgiving…. How could I not have assumed?

He took me home by carriage. My joints were jelly and yet I felt invincible. At my door, he pressed my hands to his mouth. "You are special. It's been an altogether special evening. The new baby will be a fine bond between us, Emilie. I'm tired. Goodnight."

I curled up in bed with my hands tucked between my thighs, holding back the choir singing there.

My future was clear: I would marry Gustav Klimt.

And then, except for those times when he came to visit Helene and the baby, it was just as it had been before "our" night. Ironically, Father now trusted him, and sometimes they drank plum brandy and smoked cigars in the front room.

Helene's grieving affected us all. But finally, when Helene was feeling strong enough to consider an evening out, Klimt announced that he would escort her, Pauline, and me to the Court Opera to see *Die Fledermaus*.

In 1869, when the French Renaissance opera building on the Ringstrasse was new, a critic said it looked like "an elephant lying down to digest its dinner." One of the building's architects responded to that unkind comment in typical Viennese fashion: He committed suicide. The other architect died two months later of a broken heart. "Critics strew a lot of broken glass on the path," Klimt said, "and artists all travel barefoot."

My sisters were delighted with Klimt's invitation. They knew I found Klimt fascinating, but neither of them knew that I was living in agony: *Why doesn't he come to me?* And ecstasy: *Shall I begin monogramming the sheets?*

Take my advice. Never monogram the sheets in advance.

.⁻.⁻.⁻.⁻.⁻.⁻.⁻.⁻.⁻.⁻.⁻.⁻.⁻.⁻.⁻.⁻.⁻.⁻.

The Opera

At the opera, Klimt and I were seated next to one another in the balcony. I loved looking through my opera glasses at the gowns. Often I thought, "Surely I could design something more flattering than that pink thing!"

Klimt borrowed my glasses. He was concentrating on someone in orchestra seating. When I retrieved the glasses, I trained them on the same spot. Hmm. Alma Schindler. She was wearing white satin. I was sure she could glow in the dark. "Do you think she's attractive?" I whispered.

"She's everything a man could want in a woman," Klimt answered. At this point, I realized I should not ask Gustav Klimt anything I did not want him to answer.

No, to my frustration, Gustav made no effort to draw closer to me during the second half of 1893. I knew he was so deeply depressed by the death of his Father and Ernst, that he was not painting. That I understood. But word came to me through Pauline, who still considered him "an undesirable element," that he had fathered a child by one of his models.

"I don't believe it!"

"Does the baby have to sport a balding head and beard for you to recognize the truth?"

Helene was more sympathetic. "Emilie, Gustav Klimt lives in a different world from ours. Don't try to understand. He loves little Heli and he is tender and adoring to her. Don't think about him as anyone other than a devoted godfather. His personal life shouldn't concern you."

Shouldn't concern me! This is the man whose face I kiss in fantasy on my pillow each night! This is the man who was… intimate… with some street girl on the same bed as—oh God, oh God….

My Education

For two years following graduation from private school, I attended finishing school. So now I was finished. But for what? I told Father I wanted to attend the University of Vienna. The University opened its doors in 1365—to men, definitely not to women. Father persuaded a friend who taught business and finance to allow me to sit in the back of the lecture hall. I received no credit,

I was told to wear black and arrive 15 minutes before class and never, never to ask or answer questions.

Often I knew the answers when no one else did. I was so frustrated! "But why? Why should I have to hide in the shadows and not respond when I know the answers? The boys in my class just want to fence and drink beer and swagger around with other stupid students in their arrogant clubs and say horrible things about the Jewish students. This is education?"

"Emilie, don't try to understand. Accept," Father said wearily. But when his friend, Professor Horowitz, came to dinner, I was not shy about voicing my opinions, which embarrassed Father.

"Sometimes my youngest daughter walks down a less-traveled street, Stefan," Father said, cutting his beef vigorously.

"No, no, Hermann, let the child speak. She is brighter than nine-tenths of the fools in her class. It's too bad she isn't running your affairs and mine," he laughed, looking at me carefully over his *pince nez*. "Let her come 'round on Saturdays. We'll sit and chat. She may learn something from my crotchety old age, I may learn something from her youth."

And so I became a private student of dear Professor Horowitz. We drank gallons of tea, he asked me questions and listened to me struggle, and I asked him questions and listened to him evaluate his life's work. I couldn't have wanted a better education.

The Coffeehouse

My education wasn't limited to Professor Horowitz's University office. Sometimes after Gustav and I had walked Heli around the garden and played hide and seek, he asked my parents' permission, and then invited me to a coffeehouse. There were 150 in the city—30 along the Ring alone. We were often joined by Hermann Bahr, who loved Gustav because he was such a splendid audience.

Bahr was the leader of a group of young writers called Jung Wien. His favorite subject at the moment was "the intellectual stagnation which contrasts with the scientific advances surrounding us."

One spring afternoon, Bahr was feeling rhapsodic, while Gustav sipped his *kaffee mit schlag*. "We must open up our senses, and greedily listen and perceive. And with joy and reverence, we shall greet that light which breaks triumphant into rooms emptied of the litter of the past." He spread his arms wide and waited for Klimt to agree. But Gustav's eyes had assumed that intensely abstract-but-focused look I was beginning to recognize. He was watching a woman swish by, her waist pinched as though by Gerti's clothespins, her hips thrust backward provocatively.

"She's not walking that way to intrigue you, Gustav, she can't help it," I whispered. "Her corset insists upon that posture."

"I know. That's why I undress all women in my head. I am releasing them from such torturous bondage," he replied casually.

Bahr nodded and leaned forward. This was his pontification posture. "I beg your pardon, Fraulein Flöge, but I must contribute to this conversation. The lines of the female figure are so completely disguised, that even the bridegroom at the wedding feast hasn't the remotest chance of guessing whether his new wife is straight or crooked, plump or thin, long in the leg or short in the thigh."

"Bahr, you lack imagination," Gustav smiled.

"And furthermore, women do not have the slightest qualms about artificially reinforcing hair, bosom or any other part of their anatomy for the purpose of deception, in order to conform to the accepted ideal of beauty," Bahr fumed.

"And who creates this idea of beauty?" I asked as politely as possible.

"I think we all know the answer to that," Gustav said. "I happen to think some women actually have minds as well as bodies. It's a radical notion, to be sure. But there are larger issues. I'm not interested in debating what cannot be changed this afternoon."

"Klimt, we live in a conservative city in a conservative age. Everything that is not expressly permitted is forbidden. Our fellow Viennese distrust anything new, anything beyond the mediocre. The Viennese will forgive anything but greatness!"

Klimt's tolerance for talk had reached its limit. "Fraulein Flöge and I have an appointment," he said, rising, tossing money on the table, and guiding me by the elbow out onto the street, and to his atelier. Inside, he removed my hat and began taking the pins from my hair.

"Gustav, we have to talk."

"Not now."

The Confrontation

My friend Marie was very beautiful: A superb profile, thick waving brown hair, perfect arms. For her 20th birthday, her family decided to have her portrait painted. Marie clasped her hands and exclaimed, "Who do you suppose they've chosen? Your family's friend, Herr Gustav Klimt! Isn't that exciting?"

"How wonderful! Why didn't you tell me?" A cold stone lay in my stomach.

"I wanted to surprise you."

I hated her. I hated my best friend. This has got to stop. I need to know what's going on in Gustav Klimt's head, in his heart.

I had never been to his atelier unannounced. I pounded on the heavy wooden door with the chalked advice, "Knock Loudly." I could hear my heart.

Klimt appeared, looking puzzled. "Emilie, I'm delighted. Is everything all right? Heli's not ill, is she?"

'No, no. I'm sorry, I know you're busy. But I need to talk to you. May I come in?"

"Of course. Give me a minute."

I walked into the first studio and sat stiffly on a chair. I heard his voice and two women giggling. After several minutes, the women—both with pale skin and bold, smug smiles—strolled through the room, arm in arm. I was overwhelmed with embarrassment, for some reason.

"Now," Klimt said, taking my hands.

"Coffee?"

"May I have some wine?"

"Ah ha. Of course."

I followed him to a makeshift kitchen and sat at the table, my cheeks blazing. Klimt set a huge goblet of wine before me, settled in a chair opposite, and folded his hands on the table. I bit the rim of the thick goblet for courage.

"Gustav... this is hard."

"Say it."

"What do I mean to you?"

He laughed gently. "Oh, my dear, I should have known." He patted my hand.

"Don't pat me!"

"You're right. I didn't mean to be paternal."

"Gustav, don't you know what's happened? Surely you're aware of how you affect me! What are we doing? I hear all these terrible stories, and even if they're not terrible, I just die inside when I hear any other woman's name linked to yours. For two years now, I've seen you whenever it pleased you. We've walked the entire length and breadth of Vienna, we've talked at every coffeehouse in the city, we've played with Heli, we've been oh-so-proper around Helene and Pauline, and then when it suits you, we come here, and you lay claim to my body until I'm so delirious I don't even know my name! I need to know: What do I mean to you? What are we doing?"

Klimt studied my face as though he were listening to a foreign language, trying to recognize a word here and there. Slowly, he shook his head. "Emilie, my dear, I thought you knew. No, of course you don't, how could you? I have a full-time, very demanding mistress. My work. I am obsessed with my work. With all the components of my work. And that means with the curve of a woman's breast, with the pale pink tint of her nipple, with the swell of it, with the urgency of it. And every woman is different, every woman is wonderful and frightening and no woman will ever fulfill me. Because that's the way I want it. I must be free for every moment, for each new flash of curiosity, for each black desire, for every brush stroke."

He leaned forward, his forehead wrinkled, his eyes wide and honest. "Now, if you can accept the fact that I consider you a valued friend, and I hope we can deepen that friendship forever, then we can continue to spend time together. But if you are going to be hurt, and jealous, and filled with… expectations, then I will have to withdraw."

"But *why?* Why am I not enough for you?"

"It's not that *you're* not enough. Listen to me: I cannot love just one woman. Sometimes I wish I could. Most people would see that as a fault. But if I'm to be true to my real passion, I must be open to every fire I find. Please try to understand: If you're seeking a husband and children, and if you need to know what chair you'll be sitting in 20 years from today, then forget me. My dear, my dearest Emilie, I am not that man."

Hearing this made me profoundly sad. But now I knew. "We're never going to give one another what each of us wants, are we? You will not be my one man and I will not be your 1,000 women."

"That's right." He wiped a tear from my cheek with his thumb.

"I remember the first time you touched me. It was with your thumb."

"Will this be the last time?"

I looked at Gustav Klimt. And sighed. From the depths of my soul. "No. Not the last. I think you should hold me so I can cry in comfort," I said. He scraped the chair back, enfolded me. I nestled my wet face against his neck.

We stood there for a long time.

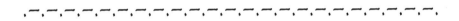

Moving On

Gustav painted a charming likeness of Marie Beuring. She reported that, "He rarely spoke! I don't know why you find him so fascinating. He made me nervous. No one has ever looked at me so, well, so *carefully*."

"I know."

In 1894, Klimt and Matsch were commissioned to decorate the ceiling of the University's Great Hall. Matsch was responsible for the huge centerpiece. The theme was *The Triumph Of Light Over Darkness*. Matsch was also painting *Theology*, and Klimt was assigned the panels depicting *Philosophy, Medicine* and *Jurisprudence*. It was a plum commission. Klimt rented an additional high-ceilinged studio on Florianigasse just to work on these paintings. First, he did hundreds of sketches. Sometimes he allowed me to stand at the back of the studio, watching him, feeling his intensity, sensing the strong, solid body move with such confident power and grace. He made the room vibrate.

Once he turned to me and said, "Midi, you are the only person I've ever allowed watch me work." I thought, "That's like another man saying, 'I love you.'" Or so I supposed.

Klimt usually came to see Heli on Sunday mornings, and after they'd played, we took long walks. Aside from these Sunday morning rituals, my life didn't have much focus. Mother and Father were waiting for Pauline and me to marry. But neither of us was interested in the so-called "suitable" men we met in Vienna.

I don't know what kind of man would have met with Pauline's approval. "Men smell of cigars and wine. And I cannot see the advantage of fetching slippers. That's what dogs are for." So Pauline gave piano lessons in our drawing room three afternoons a week. The endeavor was dignified, she was an effective teacher, and the money was a welcome contribution to the family coffers.

Gustav gave money to Helene in the guise of Heli's godfather, bless him. Mother admitted to us privately that supporting a houseful was becoming a burden to Father. His meerschaum business was failing, and Father's stubborn pride would not allow him to change businesses. Pride was paramount: Several years ago, Father's hat blew off as we crossed a bridge and floated majestically down the Danube. We were forbidden to tell anyone because it was an affront to Father's pride.

So earning money to help support the family had to happen almost by accident, and it had to be subtle. Quietly, I began to design and build clothing. For friends. And for Alma Schindler.

"You're cheaper than a trip to Paris, even if you're not as much fun," Alma sniffed. She loved expensive clothes and she could afford them, indirectly. After the death of her father, the painter Emil Schindler, her mother married Carl Moll, one of Schindler's students. Moll adored the luscious Alma, more than he did his stout new wife, some surmised. He allowed Alma whatever she wanted. She referred to him as "My Mother's husband. My Father was a saint. This one is just a normal person."

Alma required dresses that accentuated her bosom and cinched in her ample waist. These were the designs I most disliked, but she was a paying customer. I should have been paid to listen to her, too. Soon, Dr. Sigmund Freud turned listening into a paying profession. Alma was compulsively seductive, but she only lusted after men who were tottering on the brink of fame. She was aggressive with a prurient interest that oozed from her pores, somehow creating a translucent complexion. Unfortunately.

On this particular afternoon, I am kneeling on the floor, my mouth filled with pins. Alma is standing on a footstool. Arthur Schnitzler could have learned all he needed to know about inner monologues from Alma: "I know you take Sunday walks with Gustav Klimt. What is he like, Emilie? I mean, he is so intense, isn't he? I find intensity fascinating. I'm intense, you know. I've asked Mother's husband to introduce us and he keeps saying yes but he hasn't done it yet, and I can't bear the waiting! I try to minimize agony. But I think I've finally convinced Mother's husband to let me join them the next time Klimt comes to dinner. After he spends a little time with me, who knows what will happen?"

"Alma, stand still or I'll prick you."

"I've seen you and Klimt together at the Opera, with your dear sisters, of course. I keep hearing that he has all these illegitimate children. His models are just loose women, you know. And then he has lots of sisters, and he still lives with his mother. And of course, he has you to take walks with. He's always surrounded by women, isn't he? Soon, I'm sure I shall be one of them, discreetly, of course. OUCH! Can't you be more careful?"

.⎯.⎯.⎯.⎯.⎯.⎯.⎯.⎯.⎯.⎯.⎯.⎯.⎯.⎯.⎯.⎯.⎯.

The Secession

Klimt was appointed professor at the Academy of Fine Arts, but the Minister of Culture inexplicably refused to confirm him. Typically, Klimt did not talk about it. Instead, he immersed himself in research, adding an expertise about Eastern civilization to his already broad knowledge about ornamental styles from the past.

He read voraciously. And on any visit to a coffeehouse, he was welcome to join the self-appointed intellectuals who frequented their favorite tables on a daily basis. Klimt didn't say much, but other artists loved having him there. The more he listened, the smarter they thought they were. Often someone tried to draw him out. Once, writer Ludwig Hevesi urged, "And what does our Herr Klimt have to say?"

Klimt replied, "I don't have to say. I have to paint."

Finally, in 1897, Klimt and other artists began to chafe openly against the conservative thinking of the group that controlled the Kunstlerhaus, the organization that owned the only exhibition hall in Vienna.

I remember clearly the evening of 3 April. Helene and I were putting Heli to bed when Gerti came to the nursery to tell us that Klimt was waiting in the parlor.

"Gustav! Would you like to bid Heli goodnight?"

"Not tonight."

"What's happened?"

"Politics. A group of us within the Kunstlerhaus are finally totally disgusted with the petty, duplicitous behavior of the idiots who run that place. So we've organized our own group. They elected me president, probably because they knew I wouldn't have enough sense to say no. We're calling ourselves the Secession, after the group in Munich. Now I need to draft a letter to the committee stating our views. You know how I hate to write letters."

"Sit down. Tell me in your own words what you want to say. Have a cigar. That always relaxes you." An hour later, Klimt left with a smile on his face and a letter in his hand:

"As the committee must be aware, a group of artists within the organization has for years been trying to make its artistic views felt. These views culminate in recognizing the necessity of bringing artistic life in Vienna into vigorous contact with art abroad; of mounting exhibitions on a purely artistic footing, free from any commercial considerations; of awakening in wider circles a more modern view of art; and lastly, of inducing a heightened concern for art in official circles."

I thought the letter a bit officious, but it captured the committee's attention. For the next six weeks—meetings, talks, arguments, debate.

Late on 22 May, Klimt stormed into the kitchen. "Your father said you should make me tea."

"A tea evening. This must be serious!"

"The committee censured the Secession group. The chairman read a cutting reprimand. Very demeaning, very self-serving."

"And?"

"And… I stood up without a word and walked the entire length of the room. Eight others joined me, and silently we filed from the meeting. You would have enjoyed it, Emilie. It was fairly dramatic."

"Good for you! And now?"

"Now I resign."

"You can write that yourself, I trust."

"Already done. Let's see who stands with me."

"This calls for brandy, not tea."

Eighteen artists resigned with Klimt. Three others telegraphed their support from Paris. And so the Vienna Secession was born—a babe without a home.

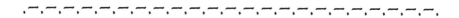

The Ferris Wheel

The Secessionists promised to "recognize no distinction between 'high art' and 'minor art' or between art for the rich and art for the poor. Art is common property." Hermann Bahr, always ready with a Statement of the Day, proclaimed, "Painting alone is not enough. We shall not have a truly Austrian art until it becomes a living force in our daily lives. All endeavors should subscribe to the concept of one total work of art, with harmony its dominant visual characteristic."

The Secessionists welcomed all artistic endeavors: The Impressionists, Naturalists, Modernists, Stylists, all were welcome. And they embraced all kinds of artists: Painters, designers, graphic artists, sculptors, typographers, architects.

Klimt was the most successful of the artists, and the one who least liked arguments, I think. The piecing together of the Secession was for Klimt a mission. But before there could be a painting hanging on a wall, there had to be a wall. So their two challenges were: Acquiring a building, and acquainting foreign artists with their intentions in order to solicit international work for exhibition.

Artist Josef Engelhart came galloping to the rescue. He knew more languages than any other artist, and so was dispatched to England, France, Germany, and Belgium to meet with every famous artist and sculptor he could find.

Engelhart also saved the day regarding a space for the Secessionist's first exhibition. Gustav and I were dining at the Cafe Marbold, when Engelhart descended on our table.

"Klimt, I'm so glad to find you. Your Mother said you were here," he panted, seating himself while the *maitre'd* looked on with pain.

"Engelhart, I believe you've met Fraulein Flöge?"

"Your servant, Fraulein. Klimt, listen, I've rented the Horticultural Society building on the Parkring. I've taken the place for three months at 8,000 gulden, mind you. If we fail, I'll be digging potatoes in Hungary. The society was going to rent the place to the Kunstlerhaus tomorrow, so I had to speak for it today. I hope you approve."

Klimt wiped his mouth with his napkin. "Herr Ober, champagne! That, sir, is my answer."

This is the sort of excitement that surrounded me. I felt as though I held a permanent seat on the new giant Ferris Wheel in the Prater: Now I can see forever, it's heady, it's euphoric. Now I'm sinking, now the ground is rushing up to meet me. Now I am dizzy and… sick….

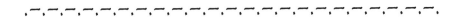

Ah, Italy

Suddenly, Gustav went to Italy. Then Marie told me she'd heard Carl Moll's family was in Genoa. I knew Gustav had by now met Eager Alma at her step-father's home. Alma gushed about the texture of his beard during one of her fittings. I fantasized lining the inside of Alma's unfinished dress with the same cloth Medea sent to Creon's wife.

When Alma returned, she couldn't wait to tell me her poignant little tale. She had chosen me as her confidante, and I expect she thought I envied her such flirtatious behavior. When she swept into our foyer, she was wearing a wrecked look. Her hair was unkempt and her eyes were swollen. She had created a meticulously tragic appearance.

"I look a fright, don't I, Emilie?" she sighed, dropping her shawl on a chair. "The most awful—No!—the most marvelous thing has happened. Gustav Klimt and I are in love. Except my parents are furious! Oh, I've been despondent for days. I know you're terribly proper, so please don't be shocked, but I must tell someone." Alma brushed wisps of hair from her forehead and licked her upper lip.

"Well! Gustav followed me to Italy. He hid behind a pillar in the marketplace in Venice just to catch a glimpse of me. I could feel his eyes peeling the dress from my body. Our eyes clasped. He made his way through the crowd. We exchanged hasty words of love, and he kissed me behind the vegetable stall!"

The most respected artist in Vienna, loitering behind the eggplants, lusting after an overweight nymphet. This man is truly demented.

Alma was stuffed into her new dress, delivering her oration to her reflection in the floor-length mirror in my sewing room. "His beauty, my youth, his passion, my talent, our mutual love of music—we were meant for each other. Oh, if only you knew how I feel!"

"Alma, you've gained weight. I'm going to have to let the waist out."

"But I haven't eaten a thing! Just sew it stronger. Emilie, you haven't heard the worst part. Our love was cruelly disrupted. I put every detail in my diary, and Mother read it and then her husband forbade Gustav to speak to me, not one word. It's just so awful for

Gustav, too. He's surrounded by worthless women. That's why he sought me out. And now we'll never be together."

"Am I worthless in your eyes, Alma?"

"What?"

"You said Klimt is surrounded by worthless women. I assume that includes me."

"No, no, of course not you. You don't count. I mean, his sisters are possessive and his mother's crazy and his models are tramps."

"Ah. I'm so relieved not to count."

Hot Bread and Jam

Meanwhile, the search for the Secession's permanent home continued. Fortunately, many of the artists had friends in high places. In Vienna, who you know has always been more important than what you know.

In November, "Handsome Karl", as Vienna's new Mayor Leuger was called, saw to it that the Secessionists were leased ground almost beneath the windows of the Academy of Fine Arts—a sweet irony—on the Friedrichstrasse.

The day after the land grant, Klimt strode into the kitchen as I was helping Heli bake bread. Heli squealed with delight and leaped into his arms. He held her, and fixed my gaze with an intensity that took my breath away.

"What have you heard?" he asked.

"Alma was here, squeezing into a new dress. Stick to your models. They serve a purpose."

"Touché." Klimt put Heli down, and drew a design in the flour by the bread pans.

"Emilie, I have a problem."

"Of course."

"Carl Moll is not speaking to me. He is one of the most important of the Secessionists. I need his support, and I value his friendship."

"You might have considered that before you played tag among the melons with everyone's favorite flirt."

"Touché again." Klimt studied the kitchen ceiling.

"Uncle Gustav, see how fat the bread is? Is it time for the oven, Aunt Emilie?"

"Yes, dear, as soon as we take the cloths off. You're telling me this for a reason, I can feel it. Heli, try not to spill flour on the floor."

"I need you to help me write a letter to Moll. A letter of apology for offending him."

"You mean a letter of apology because you molested the adorable Alma among the kumquats."

"If you will. Moll wrote me a letter forbidding all contact with Alma. Unfortunately, she described every detail of her infatuation in her diary. You—uh, you've never—?"

"Gustav, you're about to find yourself in the oven along with the bread." We stood on opposite sides of the kitchen table, staring at each other. I took a deep breath. "How do you feel about Alma Schindler?"

Now Klimt studied the kitchen floor. "I, uh, I allowed my fantasies to respond to a soft Italian night. I don't regret it. But I don't need to repeat it. Alma is, shall we say, younger than I thought. She can be very self-centered and demanding."

"You don't regret it because you're stubborn, and you're accustomed to getting your way with little cost. Heli, Uncle Gustav and I are going into the library. When the little bell sounds, come get us and we'll have hot bread and jam."

I lit the pink glass lamp hanging over the marble-topped table. Its prisms tinkled delicately. I pushed aside the dried flower arrangement under glass, handed Gustav paper and pen and ink. All very deliberately. "Here. You write, I'll dictate." Wordlessly, Klimt dipped the pen into the inkwell.

"'*My dear Moll. Your letter hurt me deeply—all the more when I think I caused pain and worry to one of my dearest friends. But I believe you are over-reacting. When you invited me to your home for dinner, I came with no designs upon Alma. I was attracted to her as a painter is to a beautiful child. You seated her next to me and we had a harmless conversation about her love for Wagner,* Tristan and Isolde *and dancing. I envied her naiveté.*' Right so far, Gustav?"

"Absolutely. How do you know this?"

"I have magic powers. Write: '*I believe Alma had heard about some of my friendships with women. I don't understand many of these relationships myself. I only know that I am often a fool.*'"

"You're going too fast."

"You heard me. A fool. '*Alma asked me questions which led me to believe that she had misinterpreted my interest in her.*' Is that true, Gustav?"

"It sounds very appropriate, under the circumstances."

"'*I think Alma wanted a little mystery in her life. However, even as a game, it was dangerous, and I take responsibility for the exaggerated outcome, since I am the one with experience.*'"

"Emilie, this is not easy to admit."

"Shall I stop?"

"No, no. You're not mentioning Italy?"

"Can you defend passion in the piazza?"

"I'd rather not mention Italy."

"So we'll ignore Italy. Write: '*Your intervention made it clear to me that one must be careful not to mislead others. I will approach future situations with clear-eyed restraint. Forgive me, dear Moll, if I brought you or your dear wife unhappiness. Alma, I believe, will not find it difficult to forget me.'"*

Klimt lay down the pen. "It's almost as though you'd already written this in your head. You know me frighteningly well, Emilie."

"I do. And I still like you, on occasion."

"Better than I like myself, perhaps. A walk on Sunday with hot chocolae after?"

"Alright."

"I'd like to hold you, but—"

"I know, I know. I have no false pride, Gustav, my pride is real. Yes, hold me."

The smell of baking bread and his cigars perfumed our hair. Soon Heli ran into the room. "Bread time!" she sang and the three of us held hands on our way to the kitchen.

The Attersee

One morning over breakfast, Father said to Heli, "My dear, why are you so sober?"

"I was thinking of Uncle Gustav, Opa. He used to laugh all the time. He's very serious now. Opa, let's ask Uncle Gustav to live with us so he can laugh again."

Father folded his napkin. "Heli, that's a fine suggestion. I'm going to suggest that he come to the Attersee with us next month. Any objections?" he asked the table at large. Father always said, "Any objections?" once he'd made up his mind. No, Father, no objections.

Gustav actually said yes. And once we settled into the gentle rhythms of summer on the Attersee, the tensions of Vienna were blissfully forgotten. Klimt loved rowing, and almost every day we took the rowboat to the middle of the lake where we drifted and talked. He was melancholy and playful by turns, and I adapted, as always.

One morning, we took the little boat out early to watch the sunrise. The sky blushed over the water. Klimt leaned forward in the boat and studied my face. "You look wonderful in this light. There is a richness to your soul I very much admire, but nothing has changed, Emilie."

"Will it ever?"

"I don't know. Don't wait for promises. And don't fault yourself. 'Don't' is such an absurd word."

The sea lapped against the little boat, and the sun flashed explosions off the surface of the water. "The sun makes my eyes water," I said.

"Mine, too," Klimt replied. He dipped the oars in the water and rowed forcefully toward shore.

Christmas

Father's business continued to fail. We still lived graciously, we just didn't buy anything new. And Father let Rudi go, and took on some of the outdoor chores himself. The dinner table was always full because Gustav supported not only his Mother and sisters, but insisted that Mother accept money as well—secretly, of course. Father's pride wouldn't have permitted "a hand-out."

Unlike many men, however, Father encouraged his daughters "to seek profitable opportunities." He was proud of Pauline's piano teaching, and my dressmaking skills. He also "permitted" Helene to keep his books at work.

"I see no reason why women can't be trained to do anything men can do. Within reason, of course." He had changed his attitude since I "graduated" without degree from Professor Horowitz's "university." The fact that we were making money was a strong argument for women working.

Anyway, one October evening at dinner we decided to make all our Christmas presents. Gerti sold me some lace from her homeland in Romania, which I added to the blouses I made for everyone. And I made tunics with embroidered panels for Father and Gustav.

Christmas eve: The smell of pine needles and hot wax, flickering candles and glittering glass bulbs from Hungary, mulled wine and firelight, red satin bows pulling loose…

"Well," Father said heartily, holding up his tunic, "I will wear this every Sunday morning when I read the papers and wait for the smells of the kitchen to tempt me to table."

Gustav looked at me with wonder. "Perfect. I may never take it off." His voice told me more than words. He waited until we were alone by the tree to hand me a box wrapped in his brown sketching paper which he'd decorated with a mosaic design scrawled loosely in red and blue crayon. He crumpled the paper and threw it on the floor. Cradled in the tissue were a superbly crafted mirror and silver brush.

"A young designer named Joseph Hoffmann made these just for you," he explained proudly.

"Oh, Gustav, how lovely!"

"I don't think you see yourself the way I do. Here. Look. What do you see?"

"A plain face. Frizzy hair. My cheeks are too fat, and my mouth is too thin."

"And I see a winsome smile. Intelligent eyes. Glowing skin. Mercurial expressions. Strength. Vulnerability."

At this moment, Father called into the front room, "Children, let's sing 'Silent Night' to Heli before she goes to bed."

We stood in a circle, Father and I arm in arm. I looked up at his profile. I was looking at a man, not just my father. He was handsome. "I wonder who he really is?" I thought. "I would like to know this man better."

My curiosity came too late. Three days after Christmas, while shoveling snow to make a path for Mother, Father suffered a heart attack, and died right there in our backyard.

Where he'd played horseshoes ...

Where he'd carried us on his shoulders...

Where he'd sipped wine at the table in the arbor...

I thought my heart would burst.

The Opening

Klimt's poster announcing the first Secession exhibition in the Horticultural Society showed Theseus battling the Minotaur while Pallas Athena looked on. Symbolically, youth throwing off the shackles of the older generation, new artists overcoming their rigid conservative seniors. Theseus was very naked. The censor banned the poster. So Klimt added tree trunks to hide the god's genitals. "I gave the censor a more virile symbol than the real thing," Klimt remarked. But the censors only saw black tree trunks, growing straight up, out of nowhere, so they were satisfied.

The exhibition opened, after several all-night installation sessions, in March, 1898. Everyone who came to the opening was driven by curiosity, speculation, doubt, or mad enthusiasm.

This was the first event our family attended since Father died. We arrived just as the Emperor did. Water-colorist Rudolf von Alt, the honorary chairman of the Secession, greeted Emperor Franz Joseph. Von Alt was even older than the Emperor. White hair glowed in the foyer.

When he saw us clustered in the doorway, Klimt rushed to welcome us. He kissed Mother's hand. "My only regret is that your husband is not with us tonight." Mother clasped his hand in both of hers. "Thank you, Gustav," she whispered.

As he took my hand, he said quietly, "And I thank you, Emilie Flöge, for your support and your patience. I don't tell you that enough."

"Many women never hear those words, Gustav. I thank you."

We walked slowly through the magnificent exhibition. The paintings were hung at eye level on walls painted matte white, red or green. Movable partitions gave the building maximum flexibility. Each painter's work was hung together, which unified the exhibit. More than 57,000 people attended and 218 paintings were sold. The artists donated their profits to constructing a permanent Secession building. The heady aroma of change perfumed the air.

Hermann Bahr, bubbling with glee, wrote, *"We have never seen such an exhibition. An exhibition with not a single bad picture. An exhibition, in Vienna of all places, which is a resumé of the entire modern movement in painting. An exhibition which shows that we in Austria can boast of artists fit to appear beside the best of the Europeans. We can measure ourselves by our own standards."*

The Emperor said what he always said, "Very interesting." During all of this confusion, Klimt painted a canvas, long overdue, for the music room of the Ringstrasse mansion owned by wealthy

Greek businessman, Nikolaus Dumba. The new painting joined another he'd finished three years earlier; it was an impressionistic view of Franz Schubert, looking round and dreamy, aglow in candlelight, illuminating an ordered society moving in harmony and peace. Bahr called it "the most beautiful Viennese picture ever painted. Klimt, you've surpassed yourself," he announced one day over coffee.

Klimt laughed. "Such praise is hard to take seriously from a man wearing whipped cream on his beard."

Later—a sensual spring afternoon—as we sat on a bench in Gustav's garden behind the high wall, I asked him, "Why don't you let people compliment you?"

He lit a cigar. "Because everyone is a critic with two heads. Comes from living in the Dual Monarchy, no doubt. One pair of eyes views you with favor, the other pair is narrowed with condemnation. It's more important to please myself than to please either the Minister of Education or his tailor. And, actually, I am a harsher critic of myself than any critic is. I know when I succeed, and when I fail. So I try to ignore opinion. Opinion can poison and paralyze one's instincts. I feel I ask myself the important questions, Emilie. Perhaps that's all one can do."

I placed my hand in his as we sat side by side, leaning against the sun-warmed wall. I do love this man.

The Motto

The Secession building was designed by Josef Maria Olbrich, a young protegé of architect Otto Wagner. The look was, more or less, Egyptian temple. Three-thousand iron laurel leaves gilded with gold formed a lacy globe crown for the building.

The artists broke ground on 28 April, 1898. People on their way to work stopped to stare as the building took shape, and those in the marketplace behind the building debated at length about their strange geometric neighbor. The glittering globe became "the golden cabbage", and people either loved it or hated it. No one ignored it.

Over the entrance is a rather pretentious motto. But the Secessionists planned to change society through art, so pretension was a boutonniere in their lapel. The motto, like so much else, was the result of coffeehouse conversation.

One afternoon, around a table at the Cafe Sperl, sat art critic Ludwig Hevesi, designers Koloman Moser and Alfred Roller, and painter Carl Moll (oh, the apologia soothed Moll's anger overnight). I was there, too. Klimt asked me to join him at the cafe before we dined. Everyone was polite to me, but I was self-conscious waiting for Klimt to arrive.

Moser was the one who introduced the subject of the motto. "The building is resplendent, extraordinary, it dances! But we need something over the door."

"You're right, we do," Roller agreed. "What about, 'Truth Is A Fire And To Speak The Truth Means To Shine And Burn'?"

Silence. Finally, Moll said, "Too long. What about, 'Art Holds Up A Mirror To Civilization'?"

Hevesi said, "No, no, my dear Moll. People will expect little mirrors all over the place."

At this point, Bahr and Klimt strode into the crowded coffeehouse. Moser called, "Hurry! We're making world-shaking decisions!"

"What could you have decided without me?" Bahr asked, trying for nonchalance.

"We think there should be a motto above the entrance. Something that will tell the world how we feel, what we stand for," Roller explained.

"I have it!" Bahr shouted, slamming his fist on the table, causing the cups to jump in their saucers. "'True Art Is Made By The Few For The Few!'" The group stared at him incredulously. "All right, I retract that. I'll use it some other time."

Hevesi grabbed Moser on his right and Moll on his left. "This is it: 'To Every Age It's Art, To Art It's Freedom.' Is that not great?"

Nodding all around. "Yes, that says it all."

"It would fit the space."

"Imagine, an art critic on the side of art."

"Klimt!" Hevesi exclaimed, "What's your opinion?"

Klimt scowled. "Well, it's not as succinct as 'Welcome,' but it states our philosophy. Yes, I like it very much. Emilie?"

The artists looked at me with astonishment. Clearly, Klimt was inviting me to voice a contradictory opinion if I chose. Blood rushed to my cheeks; I took a deep breath. "I think it's an excellent choice. And it will still be true 100 years from now."

"Let's hope the building is still standing around it!" Moser laughed. They all laughed, clapped each other's shoulders. Moser kissed my hand, and looked merrily into my eyes. "Klimt is too short and stout for someone of your grace and stature, Fraulein. Consider a more dapper man when you tire of present company."

"I suppose the dapper man has a dapper moustache?" Klimt asked, holding my coat.

"Herr Moser, I am flattered, but I have an inexplicable fondness for beards," I called over my shoulder as Klimt quickly led me between the tables and out the door.

"Why, Gustav Klimt! I think you're capable of jealousy. What a charming discovery."

"Of course I'm capable of jealousy, my friend," he growled, hailing a carriage. "Josefstadterstrasse 21," he told the driver, then turned to me, "unless you'd like to have dinner first?"

.⁻.⁻.⁻.⁻.⁻.⁻.⁻.⁻.⁻.⁻.⁻.⁻.⁻.⁻.⁻.⁻.⁻.⁻.

Crumbs

Some evenings, after reading Heli a story and settling down in the sitting room with my sewing, I felt a terrible discontent. Since Father died, I'd been asking myself, "What am I doing with my life?" Marie was now married, and that distanced us. I took a pattern designing course, but I already designed handsomer clothing myself. My "sewing room" customers recommended me to their friends, and I had as much work as I could handle, but it was time-consuming, and most of the customers were like Alma—more interested in a tiny waist than in a fine line.

There was still the question of marriage. Safe men were invited to dinner: My brother Hermann's friends, or the sons of Mother's friends. They had a choice: An opinionated piano teacher, with no need for a man; a widow with a child, who still worshipped her dead husband's memory; or a woman who might not be a virgin, with a reputation for being "too independent." We frightened them, they bored us.

And then there was Gustav. He made me feel both honored and degraded. The Ferris Wheel ride again. I was viewed with envy, scorn, and speculation. No one dared ask me direct questions, even the family. But I sensed the stinging whispers when I entered a store, and was recognized. I felt defiant, and humiliated, and proud.

One night, Helene was helping me finish a gown for Frau Wärndorfer. We were seated close together, sharing light from the same lamp.

"Emilie, may I approach a very personal subject?"

"Of course."

"Are you still in love with Gustav Klimt?"

"Yes."

"But, Emilie, he's so—" Helene looked confused. "Isn't it painful?"

"Often."

"Then is it worth it?"

"Love doesn't give one much choice. I cherish the good and accept the rest."

"But don't you feel you're gathering crumbs from his table?"

"Sometimes. But they're delicious crumbs."

That Sunday, Klimt appeared with bread, cheese, and sausage. "It's a clear day, I have my walking stick. All I need is a healthy companion, and a walk in the Woods to clear my head."

During our walk, Klimt talked about *Philosophy*, the huge painting in process for the University's Great Hall, depicting man's relationship to the universe, if you can imagine anyone attempting *that!*

"Schopenhauer and Nietzsche watch over my shoulder, so I have company on the scaffold. You know how I am: I haven't let anyone see it—except you, Midi," he said, almost shyly.

Crumbs, perhaps. But better than any other man's cake.

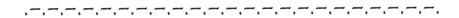

Philosophy

We've reached the turn of the century, 31 December, 1899. Many of us reflected on our past, and committed ourselves to the future. I was ready to greet this new and exciting century, stretching forever before us actively, not passively. And, paradoxically, I was filled with surrender. That's what drinking champagne does to me.

That evening, the family assembled in the parlor for music and games. Gustav always dropped by on holidays. As Heli's godfather, as family friend, as my lover—though that role was not advertised—he was warmly welcomed.

At midnight, I handed him a full glass. "To the next 100 years!" we all pledged. I felt such warmth and comfort in his arms as we lifted Heli to join in the toast. Surely, this year…

One bitter January morning, I decided to accept Klimt's invitation to see *Philosophy*, the giant University painting in process. Although I'd seen hundreds of isolated drawings of the painting, I wasn't prepared for the impact of the work itself.

Hmm. Klimt brought me a cup of coffee. "Well?"

"It's not what I expected."

"So?"

"I don't think I understand it. And I suspect the University won't either so, logically, they'll hate it."

"Probably."

"You've never done anything like this before. We're looking at pain and disease and old age—"

"—and poverty and decay and death. Man at the mercy of the indifferent, irrational powers of nature."

"I doubt that's what the University feels *The Power Of Light Over Darkness* implies."

"Do you dislike it?"

"I think it's brilliant. What I'm saying is, you are going to offend the grapefruit-faced professors deeply."

"To every age its art," Klimt shrugged.

In early March, *Philosophy* was shown at the Secession's seventh exhibit, still wet. Klimt worked on it even after it was hung.

Hevesi wrote an explanation of the painting to supplement the terse one Klimt wrote for the exhibition catalogue, but that just further convinced the professors that Klimt was subversive, and had attacked all orthodoxy.

Some members of the Secession squirmed, but as a body, they pledged support. They placed a wreath in front of the painting with their pet motto printed in gold letters on blue satin ribbon. Three days later, 87 University professors signed a petition condemning the painting.

Bahr leaped at the chance to deliver a romantic lecture: "The noise of hatred and envy, howling on the streets, reached Klimt only as if from a great distance, peaceful and good-natured, wreathed 'round with dreams. Perhaps he doesn't even hear it; or if he does, he just smiles sympathetically, for he has the assurance of all great men.

"Praise and blame can give him nothing, take nothing from him. The delights which he attains in the act of creating, when he sees his forms for the first time and, struggling with them, finally masters them, are so intense, so powerful, that everything this world can offer—this little fame, honor or miserable reward, laughable by comparison—totally vanishes.

"No, it is not a matter of him, but rather of us. It is not he who is threatened, but we ourselves. Nothing can happen to him, but we shall become the laughing stock of Europe."

"I'm glad to have you at my back, Bahr," Klimt smiled, "but they will think what they will think. Have a brandy and relax."

Only 12 professors from the University supported the painting. One, a famed art historian, planned a lecture entitled, "What Is Ugly?" His theme was that beauty is relative, and the perception of beauty has changed throughout history. Klimt had no intention of attending.

"Professor Wickoff is an ardent admirer and, more important, he's right!" I pointed out. "Wouldn't it be wise if you went? So people can see that you're not cowering in humiliation?"

Klimt was setting up his palette. "I'm too busy working on something they'll loathe even more—*Medicine*. You go. Applaud in all the right places."

Despite the efforts of Klimt's loyal supporters, the press went wild. One critic said, "There is no reason why Herr Klimt should inflict this painted madness upon us." Another scoffed, "The University professors have taken the only stance possible—with their backs to the picture."

Even Pauline was worried. "The Ministry of Culture won't accept a commissioned painting that contradicts their point of view. I'm not fond of the painting myself, but I support his right to paint it. What's that little saying they have over the door?"

I thought if I heard that motto one more time, I'd scream!

.⎯.⎯.⎯.⎯.⎯.⎯.⎯.⎯.⎯.⎯.⎯.⎯.⎯.⎯.⎯.⎯.⎯.⎯.

Medicine

The Secession published a lavish monthly periodical, *Ver Sacrum*. Klimt sat on the editorial board, which he found amusing. "If it doesn't fit on a postcard, I'm not going to write it," was his motto.

Each magazine was an example of *gesamtkunstwerk*—a total work of art. That was the whole idea, of course. An attractive young architect, Adolf Loos, wrote two articles for it. I met him at the tenth exhibition in 1901, standing before Klimt's *Medicine*.

"Your friend, Herr Klimt, will have less time to escort you to the theater from now on, Fraulein. He will spend most of his time defending his latest painting," Loos remarked.

Ver Sacrum published a series of drawings of *Medicine;* the city censor tried to confiscate all copies of the magazine. Then a Member of Parliament petitioned the Minister of Education, asking if such an offensive painting was to receive support, and therefore be taken as a sign that he wished "to make this into the official Austrian artistic trend?"

Meanwhile, *Philosophy* traveled to the Paris World's Fair and was awarded the Grand Prix. A writer observed, "Gustav Klimt is a Viennese. One can see this clearly from his pictures. But one can also tell Klimt is Viennese from the fact that he is honored throughout the world, and attacked only in Vienna."

Indeed, the current comments of the press were scathing: "*Medicine* surpasses in strangeness and monstrosity even the much disputed *Philosophy*," and, "The walls are turning and my stomach, too."

One arch critic wrote, "I should like to know what father, brother or husband were able to take his daughter, sister or wife to the present Secession exhibition and not be forced to leave the building in a state of acute embarrassment."

Loos nodded, "Yes, your Herr Klimt has made the fatal mistake of being honest. That will never do. People cannot accept naked truth. Truth must be draped. She certainly is not a nude woman as viewed from below. The poor professors will faint dead away at such obscenity floating on their ceiling."

Much earlier, Klimt had submitted sketches to the University commission. The professors raised their collective eyebrows. They said *Medicine's* central figure should be a man or a clothed woman.

"At that point, Klimt wanted to resign," I told Loos. But he agreed to make changes. And he did. He added a naked, pregnant woman. I could see why the commission was upset. They'd waited six years for this painting and now felt they dare not look at it.

In addition to the nudity, the theme was not what they thought they'd bought: *Medicine* is depicted as being helpless in the face of illness and death. The forces of fate are beyond our control. No, not a viewpoint our esteemed physicians can embrace.

"How do you view the painting, Fraulein?" Loos asked, his eyes hooded.

"I believe Gustav Klimt is the finest artist in all Vienna," I answered.

Loos smiled slowly. "That sounds very definitive. Can you also give me a definitive answer to this question: Will you dine with me?"

I hesitated only a moment. "My definitive answer is: I will."

"Good. There is a nice coffeehouse close by. Shall we stop there first?"

"You refer, perhaps, to the Cafe Museum?" Loos was its architect.

"But of course. Let's leave this place. It bores me."

Instantly, I felt guilty. How ridiculous! Gustav Klimt was, to whatever extent, involved for an afternoon, a week, a month—with any woman who crossed his path.

His drawings of women—well, I couldn't imagine lying on my own bed, alone in the dark, the way his models displayed themselves right in front of him in broad daylight!

And sometimes I suspected his models weren't just "ladies of pleasure." Women of great rank and wealth often greeted me slyly at the opera, as though we shared some delicious secret. I asked Gustav 1,000 questions in my head. But I wasn't certain I wanted to hear the answers, so I never voiced the questions. Instead, I went to dinner with Adolf Loos.

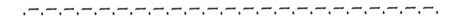

Loos

Klimt heard that I'd dined at the Sacher Hotel with Loos. He was not pleased. He sat at our dining room table, eating like a peasant.

"Emilie, I don't like it."

"I cannot believe you!"

"He's a fool for young, young women. Girls. Hell, I wouldn't even trust him with *Heli*."

"This is the most ridiculous conversation we've ever had!"

"He wanted to design the interiors of the Secession. Hoffmann didn't ask him. So Loos is hostile. Don't you find him hostile?"

"No, I find him charming, as a matter of fact."

"Do what you want." Klimt took a huge bite of sausage. Chewed it noisily. Gulped some wine. "Emilie, it looks bad. It just looks bad."

"Well, it feels good."

"The man's a dandy."

"I don't mind."

Silence. I sipped my wine and felt mutiny. Gustav Klimt wanted me only on his terms. The fact that I might have terms of my own never occurred to him. I knew this was not a unique situation. In fact, it's standard behavior for Viennese men. But I resented it anyway.

"Emilie?"

I didn't answer.

"I want to paint you."

We looked at each other across the table. Finally, "Oh, I'd like that."

"I want to do something different for you. I won't do any sketches. I'll let the work take on the life it chooses."

Suddenly, I felt shy. "When?"

"Soon, soon. After our summer holiday." He looked very pleased with himself. Hmm.

"Gustav, don't try to manipulate me, and don't try to control me. My affection for you does not prohibit other friendships. Just because you have suddenly decided to paint me does not change my desire to know Adolf Loos."

"As you will." He stared out the window. "I know I'm possessive. It's my nature. Or perhaps it's human nature."

"I consider you an expert on the subject of human nature."

"That's why I'm concerned."

"And that's why I'm flattered."

We touched goblets in mutual salute.

.⌐.⌐.⌐.⌐.⌐.⌐.⌐.⌐.⌐.⌐.⌐.⌐.⌐.⌐.⌐.⌐.⌐.⌐.⌐.

Mizzi

The Ministry refused to confirm Klimt's appointment after he was elected a second time to a professorship at the Academy of Fine Arts. Klimt's only comment: "If I were teaching, I'd have less time to paint."

And painting always came first. On the day the newspapers called him a pornographer, a circle of friends stormed his studio. "What do you intend to do?" Hevesi demanded.

"You must sue for libel," Bahr declared.

"You'd win, trust me," art critic Berta Zuckerkandl added.

Klimt listened silently, continuing to paint. "How long would an action of this kind take?"

Hevesi pursed his lips, "About two days."

Klimt looked at them with sparkling eyes. "But, my friends, I could spend those two days painting."

Later, Berta shook her head. "I think he enjoyed the scene, Emilie. He can be so infuriating!"

"Really? I hadn't noticed," I replied with elaborate innocence. She looked at me quizzically, before hugging me.

The summer holiday was especially welcome. My brother had married into the Paulick family. They had a beautiful villa on the banks of the Attersee. Every morning at my brother's place, Klimt exercised with barbells. Then he swam and joined the family for breakfast. Weather permitting, he explored the forest, stopping frequently to evaluate scenes through his square ivory frame. Sometimes he hid his canvases in the underbrush to avoid carrying them back and forth to the villa.

"Landscapes relax me," he smiled as we lay on the forest's floor.

"And not a nipple in sight," I teased, tugging gently on his with my teeth.

"Emilie, I'm shocked!" he laughed in mock horror, caught my face between his hands, buried his fingers in my hair. "Don't stop."

Every day we rowed across the lake with Heli and Trude, my brother's child. Some evenings we went to the neighboring village for a bowling party and singing in the tavern. Klimt was very much at ease with the farmers there. He was loud, spoke in the coarse dialect of his Father, roared with bawdy laughter, smoked his cigars, and drank beer. Everyone loved him.

I was never as comfortable with our tavern visits as Gustav. But last week, something unusual happened. My sisters and I were sitting at a rough wooden table in a corner of the tavern. The village called us The Unmarried Ones, but we were tolerated because of The Man Vienna Cannot Change.

Suddenly Klimt turned from a huddle of men and called, "Emilie! I've been bragging about you, about what a fine dancer you are! Prove to these manure-hoisters that I'm not a liar! Clear the chairs, make a stage!"

I was appalled. True, dancing held second place on my ecstasy scale. But to dance in front of these red-faced, rather drunk strangers? I looked at Pauline, wild-eyed.

"Well, why not?" she shrugged casually. "I play the piano in front of strangers at every opportunity. I can't see this is much different. Except, of course, you haven't practiced properly."

Why not, indeed? Actually, Pauline was wrong. I'd been rehearsing for 15 years, I just didn't know it. I removed my shawl and asked the musicians, "Could you play something Spanish, perhaps?" I have no idea what they played. It didn't matter. I was 17 again, dancing without inhibition in my bedroom with an imaginary partner! Was I actually performing this private act before dozens of strangers? Ohhh, I felt outrageous and wonderful! The applause was intoxicating. And Klimt was thrilled.

"You are the Loie Fuller of the Attersee! You must do this more often, Emilie, say you will!"

"For you, I will," I panted. Klimt knocked over his chair and shouted, "Give us a waltz!" Total seduction: The swell of *schrammel* music, the healthy smell of sweat and beer, and surrounded by farmers, clapping in rhythm, we danced as though we were the stars of the most elegant cotillion in Vienna.

I was still glowing the next morning when I took a blanket to Klimt's room while he was in the forest, painting. There, on the writing table, lay a half-finished letter.

I could not pull my eyes from the page: *Dear Son, Daddy will bring you something nice and give it to you when I see you.* I felt my knees collapse. I grabbed a chair and read while my ears rang and my mouth filled with ashes.

Further down the page the letter continued: *My Dear Mizzi, It is difficult to write. Everyone knows about everyone else's mail. The mailman blows his horn and the entire household rushes out and exchanges letters. I have very little privacy. You know how I value my friendship with Fraulein Emilie and that I am devoted to my godchild and the entire Flöge family. I do not want to hurt anyone. So please try not to write me while I am here.*

I believe you when you say your own painting is not working out. Painting is very hard. I know better than anyone, dear Mizzi. Painting causes me great pain as well as deep joy. I will bring home five paintings, but I am not satisfied. I hope next year's work will be better.

"Emilie—?"

"Oh, God, Gustav!"

"She's a fine woman."

"A model?"

"Yes."

"Which one?"

"The Schubert. The woman on the left."

"Very lovely."

"And very brave."

"God, I'm tired of stumbling over all your women."

Gustav folded the letter and slipped it into the desk drawer. "I've never lied to you. What can I say?"

"I need something else in my life. Something other than you. Something for me."

I walked out of the house, down to the lake, and sat on the dock making vague, unfocused plans.

Pauline provided the answer. That afternoon at tea on the veranda, she said, "Emilie, I received a letter from the Culinary Arts Institute. They are having a large cooking contest. But that's not the point. There is another contest: They want uniforms designed for the contestants. I think you should enter."

"Oh, yes, Emilie! How perfect! You can put your 'comfortable clothing' designs into practice," Helene said enthusiastically.

"What a splendid idea, my dear," Mother exclaimed. "Your Father would approve."

I looked at Klimt. "Do it," he said.

"I will," I replied.

The Contest

The contest was just what I needed. Within the week, I mailed drawings of a simple dress and matching apron. By the time we returned from the Attersee, a large envelope with an official seal from the Culinary Arts Institute awaited us. Well, well, well… I looked from the letter to Helene's face. "Take a deep breath, Helene. We won!"

Life became a blue blur of activity. The Institute wondered if we wanted to build the uniforms, too. I called several women from my pattern-drafting class. Yes, they were interested. The industrialist, Karl Wittgenstein, who underwrote much of the Secession's costs, found us a large room in one of his factories.

I rented sewing machines, bought material—a blue, heavy cotton that draped well—and judged accurately enough so that only eight yards were left over. The seamstresses liked me and I liked them. On the day before the opening, Anya, the chief seamstress, found me madly basting embroidery to a final apron.

"Can I speak, Fraulein?"

"Of course, Anya. I've misplaced my favorite thimble. This dratted thing is too large, give me yours."

Anya smiled and reached in her pocket, handed me a well-worn thimble. "If you do a job like this again, Fraulein, think of us. The girls told me to say this: You treat us nice and you pay us good. And you keep the lights on when it gets too dark to see."

I stopped and looked into Anya's sincere brown eyes. "Thank you. I will think of you. Even if I never pick up a needle again."

Somehow, we met the deadline. At the opening of the cooking contest, 40 women stood in front of their stoves in blue dresses and creamy aprons, with borders of provincial embroidery at the hemline. The Emperor attended the opening ceremonies. "Very attractive," he intoned.

"I thought all he could say was 'very interesting,'" Pauline observed. "You've helped add a new phrase to the Imperial Repertoire of Compliments. What a historical contribution to the Empire."

Yes, I loved the compliments. But the best part was: I knew what I was doing. I'd been preparing for something I wasn't even aware of, like dancing in the tavern. All those years of drawing and sewing, and Professor Bloch's Saturday mornings… I felt as though the pieces of a puzzle were reaching out, searching for a perfect fit, making a picture. I looked at my sisters: "I have an idea."

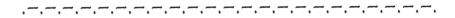

The Portrait of Emilie Flöge

The entire time Gustav was painting my portrait, I was distracted. "I don't think I was born to be a model," I sighed.

"Never mind," Klimt said, watching me with his fire-and-ice scrutiny.

"This is boring. May I see it?"

"No. Not long ago one of my commissions stole a look at her portrait while I was out of the room. I slashed it with a knife, returned her money, and sent her home."

I groaned and stood silently for several minutes. "Gustav?"

"Um."

"What do you think about the idea of opening a dress shop? Where I design the clothes and they're made right there on the premises?"

"Um."

"I have more customers than I can handle now, working at home. Of course I'll need money, and just the right space, and—"

"I'll give you money, and I'll find you space. Just stop talking."

"Why are you in such a grim mood?"

"Because I'm too hot! I could tear these goddamn clothes off my back. In fact, I will." Whereupon he threw his clothes on the floor and painted naked the rest of the afternoon.

That evening, I took the left over eight yards of blue cotton from my cedar chest and built a floor-length smock similar to the one I made him for Christmas.

The next day, before I struck my boring portrait pose at Klimt's studio, I shook out the smock and held it against his body. "Here. I know I'm probably contributing to your overall decadence, but consider this as a compromise to total nudity."

Klimt roared his approval, again threw off his clothes, and slipped the smock over his head. "Pure comfort," he purred.

I didn't realize at the time that we had just created the look associated with him ever after. Oh, by the way, I didn't like the painting. "I look so tall and thin. The dress is lovely. I wish I had one like it." The dress fell gracefully to the floor, a mosaic gown of jewel colors with a scarf floating behind my head.

"You're right not to like the painting. It doesn't do you justice. I've missed your spark. I've missed you."

"Well, it's very interesting."

"You sound like the Emperor. Maybe I should do some sketches. Take off your clothes."

"Absolutely not!"

"What's the difference? When we're—"

"No! That's between you and me. I do not want to end up on a piece of brown paper on the floor, a bed for your cats! And I would die of embarrassment if anyone recognized me."

"Emilie, you would be in excellent company."

"I don't care! Let the others frolic and wallow in strange positions and amazing combinations that only you could engineer. That is not my style."

"No, of course it isn't. And I admit to you that sometimes I'm sorry it isn't. So. For the time being, we have a painting neither of us likes much. Let's not quarrel. Let's take Heli on a picnic."

Klimt smoothed my hair, kissed my cheeks, embraced me tenderly. Hmm. "Gustav?"

"Um."

"What are you wearing under that smock?"

"Nothing. Absolutely nothing. And... I...love it!"

"Oh Lord, what have I done?"

"You've done me a tremendous favor."

And *The Portrait of Emilie Flöge*, hand on hip, watched us walk down the garden path and out the gate.

.⌐.

Alma Meets Mahler

Art critic Berta Zuckerkandl "produced" dinner parties. She and her physician husband, our doctor, loved gossip. "I am Viennese!" Berta cried. "Gossip is my career!"

Logically, then, she excelled in matchmaking, a very necessary service in Vienna. As matrimonial material, I was by now viewed as hopeless. Helene considered this my own fault.

"You've flaunted your... friendship with Gustav, Emilie. If you'd kept it a secret, you might still attract some nice comfortable industrialist. All those Wittgenstein boys converted to the Lutheran denomination, you know. And they'll all be very wealthy someday."

Yes, well, three of them committed suicide, one—the pianist, Paul—lost his right arm, and the final one became Ludwig. But Helene meant well.

On this particular evening, Berta was giving a dinner party for her sister, Sophie, and Sophie's husband, Paul Clemenceau—Georges' brother. Georges was creating quite a splash in France's political bathtub at the moment.

To add local spice, Berta invited the Court Opera Director, intense young genius, Gustav Mahler; the hysterically available Alma Schindler; Klimt and me.

"You know Alma, don't you, Emilie?" Berta inquired on the telephone.

"No, Berta. Alma knows me."

"Wicked! Oh, Emilie, you're divine," Berta breathed heavily.

Alma and I found ourselves in Berta's ballroom-sized powder room at the beginning of the evening. "Emilie! I'm so glad you were invited. Oh, darling, it takes courage to wear something that plain. But then, simplicity becomes you, it really does. Tell me, I've ground rose petals and rubbed them into my cheeks. How do I look?"

"Inflamed."

"Oh, splendid," she whispered and swept into the sitting room to flirt with as many men as she could simultaneously.

At dinner, Alma pressed her breasts into the table and delicately fluttered her fingers over the sleeve of Mahler, her dinner prisoner.

Mahler, considered a terror at the Opera, fixed his near-sighted attention on Alma and gazed at her as a rapt child might watch a large cake. When he was a boy, someone asked Mahler what he wanted to be when he grew up. "A martyr," he replied. This was a good start.

Alma rambled rhapsodically about Mahler's brilliant interpretation of Mozart and Wagner, and might he possibly consider doing *Tristan and Isolde* next spring, she adored it so. He stared at her as though she were quoting from stone tablets.

To demonstrate her compassion, Alma flushed in my direction mid-entree. "As Emilie knows, I owe my excellent home education to Mother and her husband. I've never stepped foot inside a mundane classroom. But Emilie, here, actually attended classes at University. Don't you find that brave, Herr Mahler?"

Mahler peered at me through round glasses. "You were in the lecture halls with the male students?"

"Yes. Some were real students and some were studying law."

Alma now turned her candle-lit countenance toward Klimt. Her gaze clung to Gustav's face, licked it with admiration: Oh, those luminous eyes, that trembling mouth, that heaving bosom!

The moment had arrived when the women retired to the parlor for sherry and rumors, and the men settled in the library for cigars and brandy. "Berta," I said, the model of sincerity, "do ask Alma to play for us. Herr Mahler should hear how talented his dinner partner is." Berta flashed me a triumphant smile. Everyone applauded, urged Alma to the music room, pelted her with verbal bouquets. Alma looked at me curiously—just a fleeting moment of confusion—then graciously heaved her luscious bulk toward the defenseless piano.

Klimt leaned forward. "Well done, Emilie. You didn't tell me you were writing an article for *Die Presse: The Gentle Art of Making Enemies*." Arm in arm we followed the guests from the dining room. "Let's not hurry," I suggested.

Two months later, Alma Schindler and Gustav Mahler were married in a small early morning ceremony at the Karlskirche. I found myself too busy to make the wedding dress. But I gladly attended the wedding.

.⎯.⎯.⎯.⎯.⎯.⎯.⎯.⎯.⎯.⎯.⎯.⎯.⎯.⎯.⎯.⎯.⎯.⎯.

The Beethoven Frieze

A major event of 1902 was the Beethoven exhibition. The Secession decided to honor Beethoven with a grand, brooding statue of the composer by Max Klinger, and an elaborate frieze by Klimt in an adjoining room. Hoffmann designed the space and it felt reverent, open and beautifully lit.

Klimt worked feverishly. Once again, painful hours on a scaffold. Sometimes I brought him fruit in the middle of the day. With only a week until the opening, Klimt looked exhausted, and older than his 40 years.

I threw him an apple. "You're working too hard."

"Umm. You're too late. I've already painted 'Nagging Care' into the frieze. Good apple."

Klimt combined materials: Gold leaf, casein, mother-of-pearl, gypsum, charcoal, graphite, and semi-precious stones. The result was such sensual stimuli, one could hardly absorb the entire experience during the first visit. The texture was rich, the craftsmanship gorgeous.

But the frieze was brimming with symbolism. I found it obtuse. And as I've told you, I love clarity. The theme was mankind longing for happiness. That I understood. It included a hero wearing armor who looked like Gustav Mahler; evil powers—those one is supposed to control: Lust, lewdness and excess, and those one has little or no control over: Poverty, disease and death.

Pauline declared, "Lust should not *be* a problem." Pauline's most outrageous act to date was attending a concert by a new composer named Schönberg. "The man behind me hissed," she reported, "but I turned around and said, 'To every age it's art, to art it's freedom.'" She was very pleased with herself.

I liked the final frieze panel best: A kiss to heal the world: A naked man seen from the back, embracing a woman.

"You have better legs," I called up to Klimt.

He wiped his brow, smudging it with a streak of gold. "Ah, yes, by his legs ye shall know him."

"Are you terribly tired?"

"Um. Come to the opening."

"Of course."

The evening of the opening, Mahler conducted a group of wind and brass instruments in the finale of Beethoven's Ninth Symphony in the foyer, just as Max Klinger arrived. Klinger stood stunned, tears streaking his cheeks.

At the banquet afterward, both Klinger and Klimt were honored. Felix Salten remembers:

"The two masters sat next to one another. Two marvelous heads, which bore upon their expressive faces the stamp of powerful personalities. Klinger's face, with its halo of white hair and beard, had a fiery, youthful glow, and his eyes sparkled.

"Gustav Klimt, with his brown face and dark beard, presented a picture of blossoming health, and exuberant strength. His being exuded *joie de vivre* and peace, the peace of a man who works hard, and for once permits himself repose. Here in this room was true understanding, true harmony."

This was an evening never equaled, I think. These men had accomplished a miracle. They'd erected a superb building, gathered art from all over Europe, and promoted themselves and one another—all within a framework of brotherhood and shared goals.

Suddenly, Josef Maria Olbrich stood and shouted:

"No, this is not all! This is nothing until we build a city, an entire city! Not one picture that does not go with the wall; no room that does not agree with the house, and no house that is alien to the street!

"We want to demand from the government a field in Hietzing or on the Hohe Warte—a wide, empty, free field in order to create our world, with a temple for art and craft in a grove, and around it, houses for us to live in; a world in which our spirit will dominate the entire environment, just as it does every chair and bowl. The concept is so simple and clear that one can understand it immediately. All that needs to be done is for someone to speak with the appropriate minister."

Even I, who knew almost nothing about politics, suspected that this was naïve, but the crowd shouted approval, toasted the idea with childlike enthusiasm, and basked in the sweet belief that all things are possible with faith and hard work. After all, wasn't the Secession proof?

In our carriage on the way home, Pauline summed up the evening best. "Well, now, this certainly is a night to remember. And the food was good, too!"

The critics and public gave the exhibition mixed reviews. *Die Presse* said, "Prepared by every possible means for an act of devotion, you reach the statue of Beethoven in a sort of hypnotic state." Auguste Rodin came from Paris, and found the frieze "so tragic and so blissful." Hevesi now considered this the best of Klimt's work. The statue was called "a flamboyant jewel in a majestic crown."

But others called the exhibition "a theater of pagan orgies." The critics agreed to denounce the frieze's women but couldn't agree on the particulars: One critic called them "rickety and tubercular" baggage.

"Wrong, sir!" insisted another, "They are voluptuous and spongy harlots."

Despite randomly aimed poisoned arrows, the exhibition was a success, of sorts. "It sounds better the way I phrase it," Berta said emphatically. "What I called it was a *succes de scandale*." Berta was enjoying her third glass of Apfelwein. "Fifty-eight-thousand visitors wandered through the marble maze. At least that represents a profit. Who cares why they came as long as they tossed their coins in the cup? Emilie, this is absolutely lethal apple cider. We could market this, trust me."

Although the frieze was created only for the duration of the exhibition, Klimt's friend, Carl Reininghaus, bought, removed, and stored it.

Klimt and I had just returned from the Secession, where he supervised the delicate dismantling of the frieze. "You worked so hard on that frieze, even though it was scheduled to be destroyed," I marveled.

"If I were an actor, my art would disappear forever the moment the curtain came down. Keeping one's art is never the point. Doing it is." Klimt nuzzled his cat and returned her to her kittens.

"Gustav, you have too many cats."

"Take off your clothes."

. ⌐ . ⌐ . ⌐ . ⌐ . ⌐ . ⌐ . ⌐ . ⌐ . ⌐ . ⌐ . ⌐ . ⌐ . ⌐ . ⌐ . ⌐ . ⌐ . ⌐ .

The Last Of Loos

Adolf Loos and I were circling one another. He felt that now he'd introduced me to "the corridors of reality," I would follow him down other corridors as well. He loved the role of teacher; he even offered instruction on the only proper way to eat an orange.

After dinner, Loos lit an English cigarette and watched me through half-closed eyes. "Are you interested in the erotic, Fraulein?" Loos blew a smoke ring.

"I'm not sure what you mean."

"This is Vienna. Everyone thinks about the erotic all the time. It is the most thought about, least discussed subject of our day. Let me approach the subject through a glance at art, a subject your friend Herr Klimt devotes so much time and energy to. Time and energy that might better be spent devoted to you, I might add.

"Consider this: All art is erotic. The first ornament, the cross, was of erotic origin. A horizontal line: The recumbent woman. A vertical line: The man penetrating her. The man who created that felt the same impulse as Beethoven did when he created the Ninth Symphony. But the man of our time, who, from an inner compulsion, smears walls with erotic symbols, is a criminal or a degenerate. Just as ornament is no longer organically linked with our culture, so it is also no longer an expression of our culture."

Loos inhaled his cigarette and watched me.

"What are you really saying?" I asked him.

He leaned forward and placed his elbows on the table. "I see in you, Fraulein, an extraordinary woman. One who deserves to be pampered and treated to a silken existence. One who would respond to passion with passion. I think we should investigate my suppositions."

"What is your opinion of Gustav Klimt, Herr Loos?"

"I thought you knew. I see no reason for us ever to discuss him."

"Oh, my good Adolf. You don't know me at all. I'm ready to go home now." I stood, relieved that my decision had been delivered to me so clearly. I could no more become involved with a man who disliked Klimt than I could become one of the "sweet girls" these men all craved.

Loos ushered me to the door of the restaurant, adding casually, "It's just as well we're ending the evening early. I have an appointment with a 19-year-old actress after her performance."

Loos married her within months. I just shook my head.

.‒.‒.‒.‒.‒.‒.‒.‒.‒.‒.‒.‒.‒.‒.‒.‒.‒.

The Casa Piccola

I've told you how I was led to the wonderful space above the Casa Piccola cafe. Hoffmann and Moser ran up and down the stairs for weeks, conferring, nodding, scowling. My brother arranged a license without the usual half-a-lifetime wait. I didn't ask how. Our family is very good about not knowing more than is necessary.

With license in hand, and Father's insurance money, my sisters and I set about giving birth to a beautiful shop. Now I was busier than Gustav. He climbed the stairs and watched the sawing and measuring and worker bee activities, and shook his head.

"Why are you crawling around in this dust? Isn't that what the carpenters are for?"

"Now you sound like Pauline. The workmen were horrified at first. Obviously, a woman brought the plague by stepping in sawdust. But I explained that this is my salon and my money and they do work for me. And I smiled by best Alma Mahler smile."

"That should have guaranteed you proposals of marriage. What are you wearing?"

"I made myself bloomers, an American contribution to comfort."

"You're a strange woman, Emilie Flöge. You're not even tempted to come for a walk?"

"Not even tempted."

Klimt left, smiling, still shaking his head in wonder. The next day, Helene, Pauline and I sat in the Casa Picola's outdoor café and stared up at the windows on the first floor. Our windows. Napoleon sat in this café in 1809, listening to the cannons in the distance. This will be *our* triumph!

"I wish Father could see this," Helene said quietly to her wine glass.

"Ironic," Pauline nodded. "When he was alive, we were financially fragile. Now that he's gone, we're comfortable again. Here's to insurance."

I raised my glass. "Here's to Father."

The three of us touched glasses: "To Father."

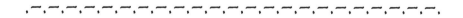

The Wiener Werkstätte

At the Secession, a post-Impressionist exhibition attracted works of Cezanne, Van Gogh, Gauguin, Toulouse-Lautrec, Vuillard and Bonnard. Klimt went to Ravenna, sent me postcard after postcard. He returned with a new mistress: The sheen of gold. "If anyone remembers me in 20 years, they'll call this my 'golden period,'" he laughed.

In May, a fabulous workshop opened its doors, the love child of three men. Joseph Hoffmann, Kolo Moser and Fritz Wärndorfer sat at a coffeehouse engaging in that great Viennese pastime—complaining—and decided to embrace a *gesamtkunstwerk* idea, the integration of all design elements into a workshop that honored the best in craftsmanship.

"How much would such a crafts guild cost?" Wärndorfer asked. Moser squeezed his eyes shut. "Six hundred kronen," he replied.

"Here." Wärndorfer opened his wallet and counted the money into Moser's hand. Moser's owl eyes grew even larger. "Don't look so astonished, my dear Moser. I'm not completely naive, you know. I've just returned from England and Scotland where such guilds enjoy great respect and success."

Within an hour, Hoffmann and Moser bought furniture and found a small flat, thereby spending the 600 kronen.

Wärndorfer took a deep breath, and said graciously, "I'll speak with mother," and three days later returned with 50,000 kronen. Hoffmann and Moser were not shy; they took it.

Within months, a remarkable collection of artisans gathered under the banner of The Wiener Werkstätte. They designed, and made, ceramics, furniture, metalwork, jewelry, wallpaper, textiles, all from the best materials and executed in the most meticulous detail. "The prices are as stunning as the products,"

Pauline mentioned as we studied smart fabrics in the Werksatte's Kärntnerstrasse storefront display window.

"I know," I admitted. "That is exactly what we're planning, too: Clothing that's superbly cut and made from the best materials. Everything is bound to be outrageously expensive, I'm afraid. I feel a bit guilty."

"Good thing we own the place. We certainly couldn't afford to shop there if we didn't."

.⁻.⁻.⁻.⁻.⁻.⁻.⁻.⁻.⁻.⁻.⁻.⁻.⁻.⁻.⁻.⁻.⁻.⁻.⁻.

A Break

I wasn't intending to holiday this summer, but Klimt said, "You're going to the Attersee, aren't you?"

"I don't know. Vienna has the most sluggish bureaucracy in the world. It's like walking uphill on sand. I really shouldn't leave."

"I want you to be with us—with me—this summer."

So my brother dealt with the myriad details in Vienna, and I lay in the grass in the country with my sketchpad. Klimt painted luscious square landscapes, and finished a full-length portrait of an elongated woman in profile who looked accusingly at the painter. He'd brought the unfinished painting with him from Vienna. The subject was pregnant and naked.

"I thought pregnancies were nine months in length," I remarked. Klimt looked at me patiently.

"That woman is at least 12 months pregnant," I said flatly.

"Is that all you have to say?"

"That's all I have to say."

One afternoon Klimt and I rowed to a secluded part of the lake. I loved standing in the bow of the boat, feeling the wind whipping through my hair, and slapping my skirt against my legs.

"Someday, you're going to fall overboard," Klimt warned for the 70th time.

"I don't care! This is almost like flying!" I shouted. Instantly, Klimt sent the boat lurching forward. I toppled awkwardly into the water.

"Ohhh, this feels marvelous!" I called, wiping the hair from my face, "Join me!"

Klimt stood, discarded his smock, threw it into the stern and dived into the glittering water beside me. Sheltered by the boat, we clung to one another, laughed, splashed. He felt like a wrestler—hard and strong. "I'd rather play with you than anyone in the world!" I cried happily.

Later, we lay on a secluded bank. I wasn't courageous enough to lie naked. Klimt was, of course. "I worship the sun, the sun worships you," I told him. The hair on his chest made tiny rainbow curls. His face was almost as brown as his beard. But even in this idyllic setting, he looked worried. "What are you thinking?" I asked.

"I'm embarrassed to say. I'm wondering if I can stand how much they will hate *Jurisprudence*."

I sat up and hugged my knees, looked down at him. "I've never heard you say that before."

Klimt threw an arm over his eyes. "I have better things to do than defend my work every time I turn around. I never want to read another stupid review, I never want to have another maddening conversation. Not with anyone. My anger is profound." He looked up at me and I saw his fragility. I stroked his forehead. "The University turned me down for the third time. I understand the Imperial art critic Franz Ferdinand himself put his paw print on the rejection."

"Oh, Gustav. How vile...."

"You have soothing hands."

. ‾.

To my Critics

Klimt continued to accept commissions from wealthy women. Most clutched their gowns with contorted fingers, a strange common denominator. Close friends bought his paintings, too. The Swiss painter, Ferdinand Hodler, bought a nipple-pink woman with a satisfied glint in her eye, Biblically known as Judith. I'd heard the rumor the model was an industrialist's wife. I was careful not to ask questions.

Bahr was bored with the Secession. His attention span had lasted longer than usual anyway. As a last gesture, he gathered nasty reviews about Klimt into a book called *Against Klimt*. He took up Klimt's battle cry, "It does not matter how many like your work, but who."

Bahr invited Klimt to dinner to break the news. "I must abandon the Secession, Klimt. They don't need me anymore. And I need to champion something new, something fresh. Don't misunderstand. I will never tire of you, but I need to stretch my intellectual muscle."

"I swim and lift barbells. That stretches me enough," Klimt smiled and attacked his tartar with relish. "Don't misunderstand *me*, Bahr. I lurch along with or without support. I've valued your every exclamation point."

And Klimt did "lurch along." With humor, with venom. Last year, Klimt exhibited a painting he was determined to call *To My Critics*, featuring a spanking-sassy red-haired woman thrusting her bare buttocks toward the viewer. The effect was both erotic and insulting. "Take your pick," Klimt shrugged.

Berta took one look and moaned, "Gustav, you can't."

"Of course I can."

"Then you are more stupid than I thought. Why give them something silly to hate you for? If they hate the work, you have ground. But if they hate your peevish attitude, no matter how justified, you're damned. They've won."

Klimt looked at me. We were at Carl Moll's house on the Hohe Worte, settled into red velvet and French wine. "I agree with Berta," I said.

"We all do!" Moll slapped his hands on his thighs. "No matter how demented the critics are, we are powerless to defend ourselves. We can break their fingers in this room, but not outside this room."

In December, the Secession honored Klimt with a solo exhibition. Eighty works. For the first time, Klimt showed my portrait. Suddenly people were pointing out "sexualized ornamentation" on the gown.

"Are those sexual things on my gown?" I asked, studying the dots and spirals, circles and squares.

"To many people, everything is sexual," he replied.

"Did you answer my question?"

"Straight lines are all penises, curved lines are all breasts or wombs. Therefore, a blade of grass becomes fraught with symbolism. I paint. Let others attach explanations if it pleases them."

Ver Sacrum, so lovingly produced, had become a burden. By the end of 1903, it ceased publication. Klimt sighed, "No matter how fine the intention, how strong the commitment, there is only so much time, so much money, so much energy. I would only admit this to you, Emilie, but some days I can barely find the energy to feed the cats."

"But you do."

"I do. And then I paint for 10 hours."

More stress for Klimt: The St. Louis World's Fair. The Secession decided that Austria should be represented by Klimt alone. Predictably, the government said NO. So Austria sent nothing. Bahr stormed, "Nothing could be more typical. When I think we have committed our greatest error, we manage to commit an even greater one."

All of this was swirling around me, but I was not paying much attention. My focus was on the salon. The walls and floor were gray felt, the rooms were spare and elegant. Each piece of furniture was a diamond—rare, precious, dazzling. I felt good. I knew Klimt was frustrated and tired. I cared, but now my own life was full and exciting, and Klimt was no longer standing downstage, center. Now he stood upstage, left.

.⌐.⌐.⌐.⌐.⌐.⌐.⌐.⌐.⌐.⌐.⌐.⌐.⌐.⌐.⌐.⌐.⌐.⌐.⌐.

The Schwestern Flöge

On 1 July, 1904, The Schwestern Flöge opened its perfect doors. Aside from my beloved Attersee holidays, I had worked for almost two years in anticipation of this moment.

Pauline, Helene and I invited everyone we knew, and many we didn't, to our opening. Klimt bought the champagne. Kolo sent bouquets of flowers. Hoffmann sent baskets of pastries.

Over 100 people climbed the stairs to marvel at the beautiful Wiener Werkstätte furniture, the dresses I made for the mannequins in the reception room, the many mirrors and the spacious sewing rooms. I invited my new employees—the women who made the culinary costumes—AND their husbands. They stayed in the sewing room, clustered together.

Alma Mahler tilted her champagne glass in their direction. "What a democratic gesture!"

"I even intend to pay them, Alma. Gerti, more champagne for Frau Mahler."

Fredericke Maria Beer, perky, full-bodied, and as bubbly as the champagne, trilled, "Now I have another home! The Wiener Werkstätte is my first home, my flat is my second, and this can be my third. That should be enough for the time being. And by the way, as long as you're going to see me minus my clothing, call me Fritzi!"

By the end of the evening, Helene held orders for our first dozen dresses. And Frau Wittgenstein took me aside and whispered conspiratorially, "Allow me the privilege: I want to become your first fortunate customer," whereupon she wrote me a draft for 1,500 kronen!

Oh, it was a *grand* grand opening!

.⌐.⌐.⌐.⌐.⌐.⌐.⌐.⌐.⌐.⌐.⌐.⌐.⌐.⌐.⌐.⌐.⌐.⌐.⌐.

Frieda

Klimt was beset with frustration, while I was luxuriating in the instant success of the Schwestern Flöge. He relinquished his commission for the ten spandrel paintings that were to have decorated the Great Hall at the University.

The issue of the University paintings was further complicated because Klimt's work was so different from Franz Matsch's. Therefore, the commission decided to place Klimt's paintings in the Moderne Staatsgalerie. Perhaps. Possibly. Probably.

Klimt was not in a good mood: "The worst part is that I can't get the idiots to give me a direct answer. Their way of facing a problem is to turn their backs on it. I've half a mind to buy the damn things back and fuck the University!"

I sympathized, but there was little I could do.

"Don't try," Klimt said. "Let's both rejoice in your success. I'm planting my garden this week. I dare the University to ruin my geraniums. Actually, I can think of something you can do."

"What? Anything."

"Ask Gerti to make me a strudel."

"Done."

Several days later, as I was taking Klimt some of Gerti's famous mood-lifting strudel, I recognized a woman coming out Klimt's studio gate.

"Frieda?"

"Ah, yes, Fraulein, how do you do?" She curtsied and looked down at her bulging stomach.

"Are you modeling for Herr Klimt?"

"Oh, yes, for some time now. He pays us better than anybody and he's nice, too, he is. He keeps a fire in the stove in the winter and we don't have to hold long poses. He wants us to keep moving all the time, moving, moving. Sometimes I run out of things to do." She was still pretty but embarrassed, and *proud*. I recognized the feelings.

"Are you free to let me take you to lunch, Frieda?" Suddenly, I needed to know this woman, our former maid and one of Klimt's models. I sensed that Frieda could answer many of the questions I had never dared ask Klimt.

"Are you sure you want to, ah, have lunch with me, Fraulein?"

"Frieda, I am very sure. Do you mind?"

"It's a bit complicated, isn't it, Fraulein?"

"Yes, Frieda, but I think we can handle it, don't you?" We linked arms and walked in rhythm to a restaurant with hearty food and private booths.

"Frieda, first, I must know: Is that you in the spandral at the History of Art Museum?"

Frieda looked at me with wide eyes and then laughed. "That was the first time I sat for Herr Klimt. He made me real pretty, don't you think?"

"You are pretty, Frieda. How, uh, how did you meet Herr Klimt?"

"Herr Ernst Klimt told Herr Gustav about me. He asked me one day when he was seeing your sister if I'd like to model. 'My brother'd like your look,' he said. So he arranged for Herr Gustav to see me. And when I met him, he didn't say a word, you know. He just walked around me a few times. Then he snapped his fingers and I turned, quick like, and he said, 'Yes. I like your skin.'

"He keeps a couple of us in one of the studios all the time. He feeds us, he gives us good wine. And when he gets bored painting the landscapes, he calls us in and asks us to… just do things. It's almost like a dance, sometimes. And if we're really tired, he lets us take little naps. He almost never talks to us when he's working, but we feel him all the time. It's like we're partners, Herr Klimt and us. I guess every one of us've been in love with him, one time or another. Mostly, we don't know men that treats us nice, you know?"

Frieda dove into her veal and *kartoffelkloesse*. I felt as though I were one of Klimt's cats. I had just walked into his studio and no one noticed me. I had become the perfect spy. But after all the years of wondering, I found I didn't want to know the details after all. Was Frieda carrying Klimt's child? Did he throw his smock on the floor—as I'd seen him do so many times—and join these unselfconscious women on the bed or the floor or the table or crushing plants in the garden or hanging upside-down from the roof?

"Frieda, I've opened a shop with my sisters."

"I know, Fraulein, I heard. We're all proud. You invited the sewing ladies to your party. Nobody could imagine that."

"I want to do something for you when your baby arrives. Let me pay for a nurse, someone to take care of you for a few days, until you're ready to work again. May I do that?"

"Ah, Fraulein, we take care of each other, the girls and me. It's a blessed good offer. And I don't resent you for it. Your kind don't know much about life, usually. Your kind of ladies don't understand our kind of pride, for one thing. I work for a living, you know? We get along."

"Who is 'we'?"

"I got a boy and a girl with my mother."

"Does your mother sew?"

"Course she does."

"Then give me her address. I'll send some very nice end pieces 'round. It would give me great pleasure to have some place to send the remnants where they'll be used."

"Fraulein, if I can say something out of turn? Don't worry. The girls all know he loves you best."

My cheeks blazed instantly. "I know that's a compliment, Frieda, and I thank you. Shall I tell Mother that I saw you?"

"No, Fraulein. I don't see a reason for it. Thank you for the meal." We stood and looked at one another with a strange understanding. "Frieda, don't mention this to Klimt."

"Course not, ma'm." She shook her head vigorously. "This talk was for us."

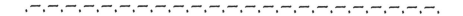

Joan Kelley

Travels

My customers still longed for Paris clothes. "I adore it, but it's not quite Parisian, is it?" Clarice Rothchild murmured, studying herself in the three-way mirror. The answer seemed simple enough. I would go to Paris and bring the latest styles back to Vienna.

I took the measurements of all interested customers. My clients' ages ranged from 40 to 70. Their husbands had money to buy their wives expensive clothes. And the husbands dressed the wives, a practice I hoped to change. Usually the wives enjoyed little or no say concerning what they wore.

Twice a year, the husbands went to Paris, and made selections on behalf of their wives. What else they may have done while in Paris in addition to visiting fashion houses is anyone's guess. Then the wives were subjected to fittings in Vienna. Whether they liked their husbands' choices or not, the wives were paraded about in whatever was the current style, to the greater glory of their husbands' social standing.

I took a model with me to Paris and bought gowns from the best houses. Then I did the fittings on the model in the hotel room, and when I returned to Vienna, voila! Instant *haute couture!*

Frau Rothchild, who had ordered seven formal gowns, was thrilled. She was delighted that she had found "this wonderful woman who's saving my husband all those dreary trips to Paris." I expect not all husbands were pleased with the new arrangement.

The Wiener Werkstätte did not have a fashion department, and so I constructed many of the dresses thought up by their designers on various coffeehouse napkins.

The most comfortable dress being worn in Europe was a long, loose garment that resembled a maternity dress women wore only in the privacy of their bedrooms. It was called the Reform dress.

"The Reform dress is rude," Moser sniffed. "Why don't you make dresses that offer the same comfort but look smart? Tell Klimt to dash off some sketches. He spends enough time taking clothes off women—professionally, of course. Let him give a little thought to clothing them for a change."

Berta insisted that I make her something that "in no way could be confused with the flour sacks the feminists wear."

"Don't worry, Berta. Style should be an extension of one's personality. You will never be confused with a flour sack."

This conversation took place as we stole kittens from Klimt's garden. If the kittens were not gone by the time they were six months old, they propagated. Klimt's studio was ankle deep in cats even with our kitten-stealing service. Berta and I were running out of friends to give kittens to. Klimt didn't seem to notice the periodic decrease in kittens. He enjoyed the birthing process, which surprised no one.

I needed to see what was happening in London, too, and asked Pauline if she would like to accompany me. Although both Helene and Pauline were partners, everyone knew who made most of the decisions, and I was self-conscious that my sisters might begin to resent me.

"I'll go providing we attend the theater while we're there," Pauline said. "And the symphony. And I'd like to go to the races. I think the British do horsey things very well."

So Pauline and I went to England and were quite taken with the suits and jackets and heavy tweed fabrics. "Why don't we have several distinct departments at the salon? A British one and a French one? And we will always have our own Austrian creations as well. Then women will have no excuse to leave Vienna."

This conversation took place as horses were being led to the starting gate. Pauline peered through her opera glasses. "I think I like the horse wearing the little man in green."

Return to Freedom

In April, Klimt decided to write a letter to the Ministry of Education, renouncing his contract for the University paintings and returning the advance with money borrowed from Kolo Moser and art collector, August Lederer.

"By now you know what I need you to do," Klimt told me while making a tightrope for Heli in the backyard. This week, Heli wanted to be a circus performer.

"I'll be glad to help with the letter. It will give me enormous satisfaction. I want you to be free of these paintings."

"It's not the paintings I need to be free of. It's the stubborn, conservative, insolent men who hold the reins of power. They usually hold the purse strings, too, as I expect you've noticed. These kinds of men rarely make the right decisions."

Klimt continued to braid rope while I sat on the back steps and wrote:

"If my work, which already has taken me years, is to be finished, I must first of all find pleasure in it, and I cannot as long as it is a State commission. I have already given up the spandrel paintings, and the Ministry has consented. I would now like to resign from the whole commission, and return the advances granted to me."

The Ministry replied that the paintings were already the property of the state. "The hell they are!" Klimt roared.

"You may have litigation on your hands. Talk to Berta. She knows about these things."

Berta led Klimt into her study. "Let me interview you. The University is not the only institution that has power in Vienna. Newspapers have great influence, too, you know that."

"I hate talking about myself. But some things finally have to be said."

"Thank God. It's long overdue." Berta grabbed a new tablet and shoved an ashtray toward Klimt.

The Klimt interview read, *"I will never again take part in an official exhibition. Enough censorship! I want to be free from all these ridiculous absurdities that impede my work. I refuse all State help, I renounce everything."*

Klimt was furious that the State played at being an artistic patron, whereas at most, it was only giving alms. *"The State should not presume to dictate the terms of our exhibitions or pass judgment on our artistic expression. The State's only duty is to act as an agent and a commercial manager and leave artistic matters to the artists."*

Since this interview didn't kill him, Klimt granted other interviews as well. The Ministry quickly returned the paintings. Six sandbags were lifted from Klimt's shoulders. He leaned the paintings against the studio walls and paced back and forth before them, swearing under his breath and frightening the cats under stools and easels.

"I could become a bricklayer. I could join my brother Georg and make frames."

"You know what Karl Kraus says?" I offered.

"That exquisite little anti-Semitic Jew? I can't imagine."

"He says that when he must choose the lesser of two evils, he chooses neither."

"I'll write that on the wall in red crayon, two feet high."

Klimt did not have time for such graffiti. He exhibited 15 paintings in Berlin and returned to another squabble at the Secession. Carl Moll was the manager of a commercial gallery, the Miethke. The purists at the Secession viewed the Miethke as a crass extension of the Secession. Secession efforts were fading in other parts of Europe; the need for art dealers was apparent.

"Almost no one has direct contact with art patrons any more. That's what the Miethke is for—to act as agent," Moll said.

For this view, Moll was forced to resign from the Secession. Conflict of interest. So Klimt proposed that the Secession buy the Miethke as an outlet for their work. The purists were shocked. They felt Klimt was betraying their principles.

Also, the Secession's Naturalists—those who valued easel painting above all—and the Stylists—those who saw applied arts and crafts as an equally important part of the artistic whole, were finding themselves more and more at odds with one another. Klimt identified with the Stylists.

"The end is in sight," Klimt told us at dinner one night.

"Well, I liked the fact that the partitions moved around in the Secession. I hope you'll take that concept with you," Pauline said seriously.

Klimt replied, equally seriously, "I will indeed. By the way, tell the cook this *beuschel* is so good, my thoughts embarrass me." Whereupon Pauline flicked her napkin at him and blushed.

Fifteen artists, Klimt among them, wrote an open letter to the Ministry of Education: *"Artists must not devote their attention to exhibitions alone, since they happen only occasionally. It is their duty to take advantage of the opportunities provided to encourage artistic life in the broadest sense of the word. No life is so rich that it could not become richer through art; none so poor that there is no room for art."*

Now Klimt was free. Free from the bickering at the Secession, free from the albatross of the University. "Come, design me some dresses," I pleaded.

"This summer. Yes, I should do that. And I'll photograph you in them so that when we're old, we will have evidence of how talented I was and how beautiful you were."

I kissed his eyes. "And how talented I was and how beautiful you were."

He pulled me onto his lap and rocked me, slowly, tenderly. At that moment, I was truly happy.

Stoclet Palais

One day Carl Moll looked out his window and saw a couple wandering about his garden. They were staring at the house intently, as though memorizing the placement of doors and windows. They seemed too well dressed to be robbers.

Moll came around the back of the house and startled them. They were embarrassed to be caught trespassing, but they burst with enthusiasm, nevertheless.

"We must know who your architect is!" the man exclaimed.

"His name is Josef Hoffmann. And you, sir?"

"Adolphe Stoclet from Brussels. My wife, Suzanne. Any chance that we could meet this Herr Hoffmann? We are ready to build a house—it may sound crass to say that money is not an issue—and we would like this man to design our house. I spend some time in Vienna, and we thought it would be ideal to build a place here so that we have exactly what we want when we're in the city."

Moll detected a *milchkuh*—a milk cow who would never run dry. Within the day, he arranged a meeting between Hoffmann and the Stoclets.

Before the Vienna house was designed, Stoclet's father in Brussels died, leaving the young Alolphe a very wealthy man. Hoffmann was terrified the commission would vanish overnight.

"Of course not! Come to Brussels. Make us a palace. The Palais Stoclet. Employ whomever you wish. I believe the Americans say, 'Spare no expense.' Put these Wiener Werkstätte people to work."

Hoffmann confessed, "If I knew how to turn cartwheels, I would."

Moser offered, "I know a dancer who can teach you. Damn! This is a once-in-a-lifetime opportunity!"

The Wiener Werkstätte, full of artists with little business background, teetered on the brink of financial ruin almost from the beginning. "I shall take a deep breath and then I shall take hope," said the beleaguered Fritz Wärndorfer.

"The heavens are rarely this bright," Moser observed, grinning broadly. When an estimate was presented to Stoclet, he shrugged, "Whatever you say. You're the experts. Just give me the best."

Klimt was asked to design a frieze for the dining room. "You should probably avoid naked, pregnant women," Moser laughed, showing his deep dimples. He laughed often lately; he had just married an incredibly wealthy woman whom he and Hoffmann met when they decorated her dining room. So he liked dining rooms.

That summer on the Attersee was gorgeous. Klimt looked exhausted from years of fighting critics, official and unofficial. He wanted to swim, to sing country songs, to dance in village taverns, to teach Heli how to fish—and, more often than usual, to find secret moments to throw his smock on the forest floor and pull me down on top of him.

But he was not working. For the first time since his brother Ernst had died, Gustav was avoiding work. Painted sketches of the Stoclet frieze were due to the Werkstätte by the end of our holiday.

One morning I couldn't sleep. I reviewed Klimt's recent ardor. I knew if he started to feel guilty because he'd not finished the sketches, his sensual and relaxed mood would vanish; he'd become morose and distracted.

I slipped into my Japanese wrapper, a birthday present from Klimt, and shivered into the chilly dining room where the sketches were laid out on the table. Hmmm. I knew his work instinctively. I've never pretended to know it intellectually. I picked up a handful of colored pencils, allowed my mind to become blank, selected a pencil… and began to work. I have no idea how long I stood there, absorbed.

"What are you doing?" A sleepy Klimt stood in the doorway, leaning on his raised arm.

"I'm filling in some of the blank places."

He scowled. Scratched his beard. "Looks good. Don't stop. You're better than I am." He turned and scuffled back to bed.

"I'm glad you're done with historical allegories," I called after him.

"So am I," he called back.

Kraus

The customers all wanted to see "Fraulein Emilie". Even if they'd never met me, they'd heard about me. Not only was I earning a reputation as a skilled designer, I was known as "Klimt's woman," a title accompanied by either a small smirk or an envious smile.

Social circles were intimate and tightly woven. There were perhaps 2,000 so-called intellectuals in Vienna, and no bridge connecting them with the rest of the city's residents. There was, however, a network that linked the two strata of society, and it was woven from gossamer threads of gossip.

People thought they knew who I was. And as long as they had written my resumé, it freed me to do whatever I pleased—not that I was repressed to the point of hysteria. Oh, Berta was friends with Dr. Sigmund Freud, and gave me a book, *The Interpretation of Dreams*. Having read it—well, some of it—I felt I could now use words such as "repressed" and "hysteria". I confess, when Berta gave me the book, I didn't know quite what to do with it.

"Well, dear, you might try reading it. Granted, you may not enjoy it, but it's not selling well so I've done my part: I bought six copies, and I'm giving them to friends," Berta confided over *Kaiserschmarren* at Demel's. "Books are less annoying gifts than kittens. You never need feel guilty about giving someone an intellectually weighty book. If he doesn't like it, that's his shortcoming, and he probably won't admit it." Daintily she blotted chocolate sauce from the corners of her mouth. Berta had worked out many of life's nagging little problems.

She was a dear friend. Close friends in Vienna were rare. As one writer said, "Friends? We're not friends. We just don't get on one another's nerves."

Sometimes I lunched with Karl Kraus, at whatever hour he called mid-day. We were both born in 1874, and this was a mild bond. Loos introduced us, and was amused that Kraus did not intimidate me.

Kraus was strange. Brilliant. Difficult. And with carefully crafted opinions about everything. Everyone knew his aphorisms:

"Austria is a laboratory for the end of the world," and "Psychoanalysis is the only disease which considers itself the cure."

"There is so much of his own misery in that line," I told Berta.

"You will never get Kraus to address his misery. He says he never meddles in his private affairs," Berta smiled, sipping her coffee.

Kraus began his satirical publication *Die Fackel* in 1899 at age 24, the same year Freud wrote his dream book. But *Die Fackel* was devoured by the public.

After three months of publication, Kraus had received 236 anonymous hate letters, 83 anonymous threatening letters, and one assault by Felix Salten, who wrote *Bambi*, a story about a gentle orphaned deer. Kraus said that Salten's animals sounded as though they were speaking in a Jewish dialect.

Talking with Kraus, one did take one's life in one's hands. Every word he selected was weighed, measured, sniffed. And when he wrote, he deliberated for hours over the placement of a comma. "I spend more time choosing the right word than many writers do producing an entire novel," he maintained.

I found myself agreeing with him one moment and violently disagreeing the next. I certainly agreed that homosexuality should not be persecuted. One's sexual activities should remain private, so long as they didn't harm others. Very few Viennese could, in clear conscience, throw the first stone in matters of who-keeps-his-pillow-where.

But I was appalled at Kraus' view of women. He advanced the theory that man has sexual urges while woman is sexuality itself. Woman has no capacity for controlling her sexual nature, and is driven by irrationality. Therefore, she cannot be held accountable for her conduct, since it is determined by her unconscious sexuality. I found this demented!

Kraus's opinion was similar to the ghastly view espoused by a very young writer, handsome, agonized Otto Weininger. In 1903, Weininger published a rabid book which became the Bible for an anti-Semitic and frightened segment of Viennese society. The book was called *Sex and Character*, a title which should have aroused instant suspicion.

Weininger said that everyone possessed both male and female characteristics in varying proportions. The masculine ideal is perfect rationality and creativity. The feminine ideal is purely lascivious. All positive achievements are masculine—art, literature, science. The Aryan race is the prime example of all that is masculine and creative. The feminine principle is represented by the Jewish culture.

He feared that, as a Jew, he would never "fit" into Viennese society and, as a homosexual, he could never live honestly. His answer was to commit suicide in the house where his idol, Beethoven, died 75 years earlier.

I was furious. I'd never met Weininger, but I felt betrayed. Live a while longer, for heaven's sake! If for no other reason than to see what happens! Aren't you curious?

How do young men lose their curiosity? Otto Mahler, Gustav's brother, killed himself at age 22. "I no longer like life. I am returning my admission ticket," he wrote. How dare he!

Anyway, Kraus's opinions often offended me. However, the last time I saw him, I enjoyed our conversation. He was holding the press up to scrutiny. He considered *Die Neue Presse* filled with hypocrisy. "It rants about the 'social blight' of prostitution, but carries advertisements for massage services and companions. To call this simply duplicitous is to lavish it with praise it does not deserve," Kraus noted curtly.

Kraus valued integrity above all and viewed an artist's work as an expression of his moral character. He sought to make people morally aware of the difference between a chamber pot and an urn.

He was in accord with Loos here. Loos's primary goal was to distinguish articles for use from *objets d'art*. "The architect, like any other craftsman, should follow the plumber as his model, not the sculptor. I would rather be mistaken for a bricklayer or a valet than an architect of our time," he sneered as our carriage passed the ponderous buildings on the Ringstrasse.

We were sharing a carriage, because as Pauline and I were leaving the salon, Kraus and Loos drove by, stopped and picked us up. They invited us to a café.

"Thank you but spirits do not relax me. Brahms does," Pauline said. "My piano expects me at seven every evening, gentlemen. I never disappoint a piano."

Loos and Kraus both escorted my wonderful sister to the door. "Please return for a musicale some evening. Brahms' *intermettzi* are my specialty."

Once safely back in the carriage, Loos asked, "Where shall we go?"

"I don't suppose you would consider the new Kabarett Fledermaus?" I asked innocently.

"The architectural and artistic dishonesty of that establishment is comparable only to your friend's paintings," Kraus sneered.

"Careful, Kraus. Fraulein Flöge may snatch the whip away from the driver and chase you to Baden and back."

"I suggest, strongly, that you limit your scathing comments to subjects less likely to invite your murder," I smiled.

"The Kabarett Fledermaus resembles a paper-hanger's nightmare, to be charitable," Loos said.

Kraus was warming to his subject: "There is no excuse for 7,000 tiles of random sizes and designs. The effect is that of a nursery for deformed monsters, all ugliness and disparity.

"The only room worth considering—the only functional room—is the lavatory. I think the attendant might appropriately wear a Josef Hoffmann-designed dress. I suggest any favorable reviews of the place be printed on the Kabarett's toilet paper, and the commode seats should bear the checkerboard print that is currently so popular with your boring and self-indulgent Wiener Werkstätte friends."

"Do I detect scorn, Herr Kraus?" I asked.

"Emilie is everlastingly perceptive. At risk of seeming repetitious, shall we go to the Café Museum?"

"Known as the Café Nihilismus these days, I understand."

"My dear girl, stick to your sewing. Slander is unbecoming," Loos pulled on his cigarette.

I was prepared: "I will gladly accompany you if Herr Kraus promises not to rant against police or military corruption, Hertzl's Zionism, Freud's psychoanalysis or von Hofmannsthal's poetic aestheticism. Nor is he to froth at the mouth should Hermann Bahr's name accidentally stumble into the conversation."

"Kraus, this may be the greatest challenge of your career. Are you up to it?"

"Your glove has slapped me smartly, Fraulein. You have considerably diminished the evening's potential for interesting polemics. But I will pick up the gauntlet."

So I entered the hallowed Café Museum on the arms of Loos and Kraus, two iconoclasts and one seamstress. One subject not on my list: Vienna itself.

Kraus knew every depressing fact about Vienna. "One out of every nine persons has tuberculosis and of that group, one out of every four dies of the disease. It's known as 'the Viennese disease' abroad. The city boasts the highest infant mortality rate in Western Europe. We are almost proud to claim it as the suicide capital of the Western World. Austria's per capita income is 40 percent that of Germany's. One out of every 20 persons is a *bettgeher*, one who rents his bed by the hour with seven or more to a room. But perhaps the most shameful statistic of all: Nine-tenths of what is commonly celebrated as Viennese culture is promoted, nurtured or created by Viennese Jewry."

"I was wrong. Vienna is not a safe subject after all."

Kraus, like thousands of Viennese Jews, was a convert to Roman Catholicism. So were these converts still Jews or were they not? Our mayor, Karl Leuger, was willing to take responsibility for the answer: "I decide who is and who is not a Jew!"

"This city has been very good to you, Herr Kraus," I pointed out.

"*This city* has not been good to me; I have learned how to survive in *this city*. We live in a carnivorous milieu. Vienna races after 'modern times' as a fox chases a rabbit. The feverish progress of human stupidity appalls any intelligent man. No, my hatred of *this city* is not love gone astray; rather, I have discovered a completely new way of finding it intolerable."

"Was there ever a time for which you felt affection?"

"The Biedermeier period: 1815 to 1848 was bearable. Values were not yet tainted by capitalism, technology, journalism or Jewish influence."

"Kraus, I think our lovely guest needs to be amused, not horrified. Let me tell an entertaining story."

"Why am I suspicious?"

"You wound me, my dear. This is a story fit for the most sensitive child at bedtime:

"*There was once a saddler, a good, industrious craftsman. He made saddles which had nothing in common with the saddles of previous centuries, nor with Turkish or Japanese saddles. In other words, modern saddles, although he didn't know it. All he knew was that he made saddles.*

"*Then one day a strange movement came to town. It was called Secession. It demanded that objects of everyday use should only be produced in the 'modern' manner.*

"When the saddler heard this, he took one of his best saddles and went to one of the leading members of the Secession. 'Herr Professor! I have heard about your demands. I, too, am a modern man. I, too, should like to work in the modern style. Tell me: Is this saddle modern?'

"The Professor examined the saddle, and then gave the craftsman a long lecture consisting of words such as 'Arts and Crafts', 'individuality,' and 'Hermann Bahr'. The answer was, however, 'No, this is not a modern saddle.'

"Filled with shame, the craftsman left. Thought and toiled and thought some more. But however much he tried to meet the lofty demands of the Professor, he could only succeed in producing the same old saddles.

"In despair, he returned to the Professor and told his tale of woe. The Professor examined the man's attempts and said: 'My dear fellow, it's simply imagination you're lacking.' Yes, that was it! He had no imagination! He hadn't even known that one needed imagination to make saddles. If he had imagination, he would doubtless have become a painter or a sculptor or a poet or a composer.

"But the Professor said, 'Come back again tomorrow. After all, that's what we're here for, to promote industry, implant new ideas. I'll see what we can do.'

"And he set his class the project: Design for a Saddle. The next day, the saddler came again. The Professor showed him 49 designs for saddles.

"For a long time, the craftsman looked at the designs and light gradually dawned in his eyes.

"Then he said, 'Herr Professor! If I knew as little about riding and horses and leather and craftsmanship as you, then I'd have your imagination!'

"And he lived happily ever after. Making saddles. Modern saddles? He didn't know. Saddles!"

"Adolf, you tricked me. But I applaud your performance."

"Have I your permission to tell one more?"

"I only wish I'd known you possessed this talent when my niece Heli was younger."

"I suppose you read her *Bambi*," Kraus said scornfully.

"Until the binding fell apart."

Loos spread his hands on the table and leaned forward. "*This is the story of a poor rich man. He had a great deal of money, and decided to hire an architect to bring Art into his home. The architect's first move was to throw out everything, and design new. He designed even the smallest items. And none of them was allowed to be moved—not one inch—from where the architect placed them.*

"*One day, the architect came to visit the rich man unexpectedly. The man greeted him warmly, but saw immediately that the architect was crimson with rage. 'Look at your slippers!' he roared.*

"*The rich man breathed a sigh of relief. 'My dear architect, surely you remember. You designed these slippers yourself.'*

"'*Certainly I did!' thundered the architect. 'But I designed them to wear in the bedroom, not the living room!'*"

I applauded, my gloved hands making dull thumping sounds. "I am indeed entertained. Herr Loos, you told me once when we were together that you had a late engagement with a young actress. Well, I have a late engagement with a painter in his prime. So if you will kindly find me a carriage…"

"Emilie is ridiculously loyal. A detestable trait when it frustrates my own designs. So be it. Kraus?"

"I see a disciple of mine. I will stay and test his defense of a certain column in the latest *Die Fackel*. Good evening, Fraulein."

I stood and turned to face the little man with the dazzling blue eyes and pinched face. "Herr Kraus, how sad to be so upset about so many things. And so prejudiced. You are often completely right, I have no doubt, and often completely wrong. Winning an argument doesn't mean you're the Prince of Light.

It simply means that either you have not met your match, or you have logic on your side, and logic frequently lies. Good night."

Loos shrugged in mock despair. "Don't blame me, Karl. She hems skirts—that's all I know."

Schiele

Klimt was helping me repot geraniums. "A strange boy came to see me today."

"In what way strange?"

"Student from the academy. Uncanny eye. Bold, daring. Gives you no choices. You see his work as it is."

"Hand me that trowel. He came to the studio?"

"Marched right in. Pushed his portfolio right in my face. Couldn't be more than 17. Dark, brooding. Women will fear him a little, I think. That should make him irresistible. All he said was, 'Look at this.'"

"That's direct."

"I was amused at his audacity. So I leafed through these remarkable drawings for about 10 minutes. Neither of us said a word. He stared at me the whole time. Finally, he said, very matter-of-factly, 'Do I have any talent?' I handed back the portfolio and said, 'Much too much.' He grinned and announced, 'My name is Egon Schiele. I intend to be great, like you.' I laughed all afternoon."

"What this boy lacks in manners, he makes up for in chutzpah, as our Jewish friends say."

"He does. He does. I like him. He could be right. He's insufferably conceited. But we'll see what lessons life teaches him.

At age 50, he may be a bit more humble. You know, red geraniums are one of Nature's better ideas."

The Decision

My gaze wandered about Klimt's atelier in the gathering dusk. Leaning against the wall was an extraordinarily complex portrait of Adele Bloch-Bauer. "Tell me about that one," I said as Klimt pulled my blouse from my shoulders.

"I may have experimented enough with the golden motif," Klimt scowled. "The subject feels I lost her somewhere in the painting."

"Hmm. Rather a neurotic looking woman."

"Ever since you read that Freud book, you've tossed about these strange new words," he mumbled, tracing my collarbone with his index finger.

"Is she nervous, unpredictable, irrational, demanding and depressed?"

"Umm." Klimt knelt to unfasten my skirt.

"Does she really contort her hands that way?"

"Sometimes."

"I hear you really like her. Do you really like her?"

"Emilie—" He circled my navel with his tongue.

"And who is that, on the easel?"

"*Danae.*"

"Quite the lovely model."

"That model has more intelligence in her buttocks than most people have in their faces." He pulled my skirt down to my ankles.

"She is wearing the most ecstatic expression I've ever seen."

"If only you knew how you look sometimes.... She's just been impregnated by Zeus."

"Gustav..."

"Ummm."

"I'm pregnant."

Klimt looked up at me with such amazement and joy. I've never seen such a beautiful expression. And I'd never, never felt such ice and fire, such numbness and agony.

Pressing his head to my breast, he carried me to the couch, lay me on the drawings, curled his body against mine. He was shaking with exultation.

"Gustav, we have to talk."

"Not now."

"No, you always say that. Now, it must be now! Gustav, listen, listen to me. I have clawed the sheets at night, trying to make this clear to myself. This is what I know: I am not one of your models. I am not Mizzi, who still lives alone in a tiny hot flat with a youngster bearing your name."

"How do you—?"

"Never mind. I am not a married socialite who can claim a child as her husband's son. I am an independent, highly competent, strong woman. And I love you as light loves morning or whatever, whatever—but I cannot have your child unless I'm married to you. And I will not ask you to marry me. No, let me finish. I want this child as much as I crave the air I breathe. But I will only have this child as Frau Gustav Klimt."

At the end of 10 seconds of silence, we both knew the answer. Klimt laid his face on my stomach. "Emilie, Emilie, Emilie," he moaned. He sat up and looked toward the barely visible garden. I felt his misery swelling. The roar came from his bowels. He staggered to his feet, paced the room, beat his thighs with his fists.

I couldn't bear his pain. We gathered each other in, wept incoherently, and made love tenderly, sadly, with infinite devotion.

Seven days later, I lay on the same couch. Gustav watched over me with exquisite care. "How do you feel?" he asked gently.

"Sometimes I wish I could leave you," I replied weakly.

"I know. Rest. It would be so much easier if all our needs were the same," he said, blotting the perspiration from my forehead.

"I wanted this baby, Gustav," I whispered.

"So did I." He clasped my hand to his mouth. I felt the warm tears trickle between my fingers. "Can you forgive me?"

"Not... entirely."

Safe, Sane, Successful

For the next few months I kept very busy. My trips to the Paris shows in late February and early August had become ritual. While there, I often lunched with Carla Rilke. She spoke of her husband's fascination with Cezanne, and the color blue.

I was only superficially interested. At the Grand Hotel each evening, as many as seven postcards awaited me. All from Klimt. All about the weather. Or train schedules. None of them said, "Emilie, I love you. Emilie, don't leave me."

Very deliberately, I decided to leave him. But I realized that first, I had to be involved with someone else. I knew that was the coward's way out. I didn't care.

The problem was: I didn't know anyone who peeled my skin away. Clearly, the new man shouldn't be Austrian. Any Austrian would know about Klimt. I decided the new man should be an American. A safe, sane, successful American. Someone sweet who adored me and didn't get in my way. Many of my friends had lived in America—Hoffmann, Loos. They described Americans as simple and sincere. Those qualities sounded comforting to me. I wanted a man I could relax with.

No sooner had I created this fantasy man almost the opposite of Klimt, than I found one. During my next trip to Paris, Carla introduced me to a Mister Bill Gentry. He was a rancher and businessman from Dallas—which was either a city or a state, I wasn't sure.

Carla said he'd bought a first edition of Ranier Maria Rilke's poetry, signed and beautifully bound. That seemed a good sign. We saw each other every day for two weeks.

"You are, without a doubt, the prettiest little thing I ever did see," Mr. Bill Gentry said, melting into his oysters at a little café on the Rive Gauche.

"No one has ever said that to me before," I admitted.

"Then somebody's not been payin' attention. You shouldn't have to lift a finger. You should have servants with feather fans keepin' you cool all day and diamonds the size of gopher holes in your earlobes at night."

"What are gopher holes?"

"Let me rephrase that. You deserve the best, in every way. I don't mind tellin' you, I can give you the best. Anything your heart desires. I got lucky."

"Lucky?"

"My Daddy bought a lotta real estate in Texas. Happens to have oil on it. Add a lotta cattle to that and you can name your poison."

"Poison?"

"Miss Emilie, I'm not expressing myself well, I know, and I regret that. Here –" Bill Gentry held an oyster to my lips. "You've got me eatin' out of your hand, too, you know."

"Mr. Gentry, you are very dear. I like you, too. I think we should investigate your suppositions."

"Beg pardon?"

"Let's know one another."

"Biblically speaking?"

"I'm not sure we need to include the Bible."

"I'm Protestant. I hope that won't be a problem."

"Actually, my family is Protestant, too. Only about three percent of Austrians are, you know."

"Prob'ly no Baptists."

"Probably not."

"We got us a little cultural gap here, but don't worry, we'll work that out. Americans like challenges. Let me pay this bill here and then we can vamoose."

"No one has ever asked me to vamoose before. Is vamoosing fun?"

"Nothin' in the world's as much fun as vamoosin', believe me."

Bill Gentry held my chair and looked at me with humor and affection. "Golly, you're pretty. I love the way you talk, and I love the way your clothes move. I'd be so proud to show you off back home. Everybody'd turn green."

"Is this a desirable color to turn?"

"Just keep teasin' me. With you on my arm, I'd be the envy of the whole United States of America."

I looked at the tall, lean, curly haired man with such a quick smile, such an open, happy face. I wasn't sure how much my feeling for this man with oil wells and a truly different language was of my own design, and how much was dictated by nature.

"Emilie—may I call you that?—let me prove how much I care."

This I understood. And I understood his body. In his hotel room he was graceful and subtle in a way I hadn't expected. I felt I should prepare him.

"Bill Gentry, I may not be who you think I am. You are not the first man I have shared this act with."

Bill Gentry chuckled softly and picked me up under my arms. "Hitch your legs around my waist. Yeah. Now we're gonna get somethin' straight here." And we sat down, coupled in this strange way.

"Emilie, you're what—32, 33 years old? Not what we call a spring chicken. I've never seen the virtue in a spring chicken. I want my woman to be savvy. That means I want her to know her way from the house to the barn. So far, there isn't a thing I've learned about you that makes me appreciate you less. You didn't have to volunteer that confession. You're a courageous lady. That says to me you're honest as well as beautiful. You speak to my soul, darlin'. Now let's not talk for a while."

Much later, as we lay side by side, aglow with perspiration, he gently lifted strands of hair from my face. "There would never be another woman for me, Emilie Flöge. Did I say that right? Flöge? Talk doesn't matter now. Takin' care of you is all that matters from now on."

Oh God, I wasn't pretending. I was feeling glorious joy with someone other than Gustav Klimt. And I was frightened.

Bill Gentry followed me to Vienna. He checked into the Imperial Hotel and made it clear that he was "diggin' in my heels."

He brought armloads of flowers to Mother, fixed the kitchen sink for Gerti, listened attentively to Pauline play the piano, winking at me when she announced, as though to an audience of 500, "And for my encore—"

He taught Heli the rudiments of a game called football, which resulted in much shouting and something called "huddles" in the backyard.

Helene was the first to mention it. "So what are you planning to do?"

"Do?"

"Don't be coy. The man clearly intends to loiter about Europe until you agree to marry him, and return to his cows and—what is it?—cactus. Emilie, do you have any idea what you've done? You've knocked the entire lid off Pandora's box!"

"We haven't discussed marriage."

"But I think we should," Bill Gentry grinned from the dining room doorway. He wiped his red face with a handkerchief, tossed me his football. The orange curls matted against his forehead. He wore white trousers and wide suspenders and a blue shirt. He was quite dashing. He was quite American. I was quite confused.

Heli was captivated, but she saw complications. We were snapping beans on the back porch. Heli was snapping her beans with unnecessary vigor. "Heli, what's wrong?"

"Aunt Emilie, are you going to marry Herr Gentry, and go to live in Texas?"

"Texas?"

"That's where Dallas is. Texas is almost as big as the Austro-Hungarian Empire, Herr Gentry says."

"That may be a slight exaggeration. Heli, dear, this is all very premature. I couldn't just leave the Schwestern Flöge. I wouldn't. And I couldn't leave the family or *you!*"

"And you can't just leave Uncle Gustav, either, can you?"

"My darling, that's… well, your uncle is another subject altogether."

"How long have you known Uncle Gustav?"

"Seventeen years."

"And how long have you known Herr Gentry?"

"Six weeks."

"Hmm."

"Heli, you sound just like me!" Oh, God, oh, God….

.⌐.⌐.⌐.⌐.⌐.⌐.⌐.⌐.⌐.⌐.⌐.⌐.⌐.⌐.⌐.⌐.⌐.⌐.⌐.

Bitte

Saturday night, after Bill Gentry dropped me off, I couldn't sleep. My intention was not to fall in love with this man. He was supposed to cleanse my blood, not change my name. And yet, love waited right outside the open door. But compromise was not far away, either.

"Bill, listen to me. I have a very successful business. I started it from a bare room and a handful of patterns. I can't just leave it. People depend upon me."

"We'll send them money until they find work someplace else. I'm a wealthy man, Emilie. We can send your mother money, too, as much as you want. And Heli can go to college in America. Lotsa good schools for girls on the East Coast."

"You don't understand. I love my work. *Love* it!"

"I'll open a store for you in Dallas. Won't even matter if it makes money, just so you're happy. And we can go to Paris once a year and you can buy clothes to your heart's content."

"Bill, how can I make you see that my shop is just as important to me as your ranch is to you."

"Once we have a family, that'll be your work. Look. I bought you some perfume. Let's find new places to dab it on… "

I didn't hear the banging early Sunday morning. Then Gerti appeared in my room. "Herr Klimt, Fraulein. With a kitten."

I groaned, struggled to the door. Yes, there was Klimt holding a forlorn black and white kitten.

"It needs a home."

"Gustav, I'm not even awake yet."

"May I come in?"

"Well—"

"Heli told me she thought she could find this kitten a home. If you marry this American, I'll kill him!"

"Come in, come in. I'll make coffee." I stroked the kitten. She bit me. "This is a bad-tempered animal! Like you!" Klimt picked up the coffee cup on the table and threw it against the wall.

"Does that mean you won't be needing cream and sugar?"

He kissed me so hard I tasted blood.

"How… dare… you!"

"Please, please, please don't. I can't promise you anything. But hear me: Everything we know about one another was won with the juices squeezed out of our bone marrow. When I sweat, I taste the salt of your body. When I paint, I bask in the colors of your eyes, your hair, your flesh. When I lie with another woman, I return to the bounty of your spirit. Please don't do this!"

"Don't leave you!"

"Yes!"

"Say it!"

"Don't leave me!"

Goodbye. Goodbye to a proper life of teas and clubs and embroidery, of huge skies and laughing children with pet dogs. Goodbye to the smell of leather and bone china comfort in a foreign cowboy land.

About this, I was not brave. I sent a letter to Bill Gentry's hotel. I grabbed clothes and left a note for Helene. And for the first time in our lives, Gustav Klimt and I slipped away together for a week. Still, no promises, but deeper passion, which must be what I really wanted. I traded something called "a spread" in Texas with a sweet, sane, successful man, for my always erratic, sometimes erotic, life with Klimt. I should stop complaining.

I adopted the kitten. I called her *Bitte*.

PART TWO

Vorbei!

Alma Mahler loved being married to a famous man. But I wondered if she loved being married to Gustav Mahler. "He won't let me wear my hair up, because he says I look too Jewish. Which is irritating because *I'm* not Jewish—*he* is!" she complained one day in the shop.

Alma was one of Pauline's hat customers. "A head is not complete without a hat," was Pauline's motto.

Alma considered her famous husband "not just inflexible, rigid. And the opera drives him to distraction. You know I write music. Well, he told me right before we were married that he wanted a wife, not another composer in the family.

"And do you know something, Emilie? I'm not sure I like his music. It's not always… pretty. One symphony has hammers and cow bells in it. But everyone expects me to sit in my box and smile and flutter my fan and gaze adoringly at the great Gustav Mahler throughout every opening. Whereas the truth is, I'm usually bored. Do you keep any absinthe around here?"

"Of course, just for you, Alma," I said, fetching the sugar and spoon and bottle from the cupboard. I handed her a cut-glass goblet.

Alma scowled. "On the other hand, he's a good father, in his way. In fact, I think he likes the girls better than I do. Being a mother is not instinctually satisfying. They spit up and cry for no reason and they're not companions at all. The nanny brings them to see me once a day, but still, they look at me like I'm a stranger. Be glad you don't have to deal with these problems.…

"Sometimes I long for the life I used to lead—with my wonderful figure, and parties where young men brought me champagne, and whispered in my ear, and sent me flowers the next morning."

Carefully, I placed a sugar cube on the slotted spoon, and slowly poured the absinthe over the sugar and into the goblet. Alma watched me closely, and as her hand closed around the stem, she suddenly smiled her most radiant smile. "Could Pauline make me a hat this color? With an abundance of feathers?"

In several months, Gustav Mahler's life collapsed. His older daughter, Maria, died of scarlet fever and he was told he had a serious heart condition. He resigned from the Court Opera and accepted the directorship of the Metropolitan Opera Company in New York City.

Klimt and Mahler had grown fond of one another over the past several years. Mahler chose to ignore any ancient rumors linking Klimt and Alma. He was too busy fighting with various factions at the opera to worry about ancient gossip.

In early December, 200 people gathered at the Westbahnhof to see Mahler and Alma off to America. Mahler, usually so brusque, moved through the crowd, shaking hands, touching faces, nodding. When he came to Gustav, they embraced. They clung to one another for a long moment, bound by friendship and genius and grief.

The Paris Express hissed, then began its rhythmic pull out of the station. We waved, shouted good wishes. Then all was silent. No one spoke. Two hundred people huddled in the cold, waiting for a signal of some kind. It was Klimt who broke the silence.

"*Vorbei!* It's over."

That's all that needed to be said. We filed from the train station slowly, as though returning home from a funeral.

Several months later, Alma sent me a postcard from a place called Niagara Falls. She reported that when Mahler saw the Falls, he exclaimed, "Finally a fortissimo!"

.⁻.⁻.⁻.⁻.⁻.⁻.⁻.⁻.⁻.⁻.⁻.⁻.⁻.⁻.⁻.⁻.⁻.⁻.

Kunstschau, 1908

Klimt spent the first part of 1908 painting ten hours a day, and organizing an enormous art show—the Kunstschau. It was the first such effort since the Klimpqruppe left the Secession. Hoffmann erected a prefabricated pavilion for the show in a field, a five-minute stroll from the Secession. In addition to 54 exhibition rooms, the pavilion boasted gardens, a café and an outdoor theater.

The show opened in May. Over the entrance were the words, *To Every Age Its Art, To Art Its Freedom.*

"Hmm," Hevesi mused. "Haven't I read that somewhere before?"

Pauline poked him with the point of her parasol. "Why, I'm surprised at you! That's the phrase somebody made up for the front door of the Secession. Surely you remember!" she chided.

"Ahh, yes, Fraulein Flöge," he said soberly. "I do seem to recall. It was the jab of your parasol that refreshed my memory."

Klimt was asked to give the opening address. "I know what I want to say. But, as usual, the thought of writing it nauseates me. I feel as though I were about to be seasick."

Klimt scrawled "HELP" with blue crayon on a sheet of Japanese rice paper, across the sketch of a naked woman showing us a part of her anatomy most women took great care to conceal.

"Then let's negotiate. Design a couple of dresses, and I'll help you put your thoughts on paper. Fair?"

"Definitely fair."

The following Sunday, armed with a picnic hamper and writing materials, Klimt and I set up shop in the Vienna Woods and worked all afternoon, sprawled on a blanket. Our only interruption was a slender bearded man wearing a Tyrolean costume, complete with a chamois brush springing from his green hat. He also wore a frown. When he saw us, he stopped and announced darkly, "The mushrooms in these Woods are appreciatively inferior to those in Switzerland."

Klimt nodded sympathetically. The man bowed smartly and stomped further into the Woods.

"Gustav, I think that was Dr. Freud."

"I was not tempted to tell him any secrets."

On the first day of the Kunstschau, the crowd gathered in the outdoor theater for the opening ceremony. Many women were wearing Schwestern Flöge gowns. I was proud of that. Pauline, as usual, summed up my feelings: "When we attended the opening of the Secession 11 years ago, the women were not nearly so well dressed."

Klimt strode on stage. Looked out over the audience. Found me. Stroked his beard once—our signal that all was well and his stage fright was under control.

"We do not regard an exhibition as the ideal way of establishing contact between artist and public. For instance, the execution of large-scale public commissions would be infinitely preferable for this purpose. But as long as public life continues to occupy itself predominantly with political and economic matters, exhibitions are the only means that remain open to us.

"We must, therefore, be grateful for that public and private support which has enabled us, on this occasion, to make use of this means and demonstrate that we have not been idle during these exhibitionless years. That on the contrary—perhaps because we have been free from the cares of arranging exhibitions—we have been working all the more industriously, inwardly, on the development of our ideas.

"We do not belong to any association, any society, any union. We are united, not in any compulsory manner, but simply for the purpose of this exhibition, united in the conviction that no aspect of human life is so unimportant that it does not offer possibilities for artistic endeavor. In the words of the leader of the Arts and Crafts Movement in Scotland, William Morris, even the most insignificant object, if perfectly made, helps to increase the sum total of beauty on this earth.

"No less broadly conceived than the term 'art' is the term 'artist'. Not only he who creates, but also he who enjoys merits this title, if he is capable of judging and experiencing the work of art in emotional terms.

"Therefore our opponents attempt to combat the modern movement in art in vain. Theirs is a struggle against growth, against becoming—against life itself.

"True, we who have worked in preparing this exhibition will, once it's opened, separate and go our own individual ways. But perhaps in the foreseeable future we shall find ourselves united again in some quite different association. Whatever the case, our trust is in each other.

"I wish to thank all concerned for their efforts, their cheerful self-sacrifice, their devotion. I thank, too, all our patrons and supporters who have enabled us to mount this exhibition. By inviting you, honored guests, to undertake a tour of this building, I declare the *Kunstschau Vienna 1908*... open."

Heli spontaneously jumped to her feet, applauding madly. Her sweet enthusiasm was contagious. The standing ovation was more in tribute to Klimt than in celebration of the Kunstschau. He was stunned. He nodded to different groups in the audience, and strode offstage.

The exhibition featured a room of children's art, three rooms of theater sets by Roller and Czeschka, one room filled with products of the Wiener Werkstätte. There was a room for posters, examples of Jugendstil and sacred art, and a two-story Hoffmann-designed cottage for sale through the catalogue.

One room was devoted to Klimt. Three female portraits commanded attention. A hostile critic disliked Klimt's approach for the same reasons I liked it. He conceded that Klimt was "a master of an extraordinarily developed technique. And what does he use it for? In order to paint a mixture of peacocks' tails, mother of pearl, silver scabs, tinsel and snails' paths!"

The Three Stages of Woman was shown for the first time. Heli studied the ancient woman on the left. "It's better not to get old," she remarked.

"Your Uncle Gustav gives older models more work than any other artist in the city."

"And fat ones, and thin ones, too. He just likes women, doesn't he, Aunt Emilie?"

"You might say that, yes, dear."

"I don't think many men do."

"How do you know that, Heli?"

"I watch. I listen."

The beautiful *Danae* irritated a press critic: "Danae is rolled up like a bundle of old washing and in this position, which no woman in the world has ever assumed of her own free will, she permits us to admire her thigh and half her bosom. The rest is, as usual, filled in with mother of pearl and peacocks' fans. I can't help it, I think it's unhealthy."

Klimt laughed. "That particular model is exceptionally healthy. Our pale and trembling scribe will never have the good fortune to luxuriate in her extraordinary stamina."

Heli looked at her uncle quizzically. "What does that mean, Mother?" (Ahhh, watching and listening, indeed!)

Helene glared at Klimt. "I would appreciate a modicum of discretion, Gustav."

"Heli, I meant that the model has a new vehicle—a bicycle. And she rides around Vienna frightening the horses and squawking her horn at old men and causing quite a fuss. From all this exercise, she has developed great stamina." He looked at Helene triumphantly.

"Oh, I would love to have a bicycle. Mother, may I? Aunt Emilie could make me bloomers to wear, just like hers. May I?"

Helene glared at Klimt. "Now see what you've done!"

Helene marched into the next exhibition room. This particular room, however, was no comfort at all. Oskar Kokoschka held the room hostage. It was christened the chamber of horrors. Hevesi called Kokoschka "our chief wild animal" which pleased the 22-year-old boy greatly.

He almost was not allowed to exhibit, despite Czeschka's support. Last week, when the jury was prowling the exhibit to determine what works should be eliminated, Kokoschka made a human star in the doorway, and refused to move.

Klimt, who headed the jury, slowly made his way through the irritated group of jurists. He placed his hand on the boy's shoulder, and said calmly, "May I handle this?"

Kokoschka was confused but sensed that Klimt was his only ally and his best defense. "We've never even met," Kokoschka said in awe.

"We're meeting now." Klimt confronted the jurists. "Our duty is to give an artist of outstanding talent the opportunity to express himself. Oskar Kokoschka is one of the greatest talents among the younger generation. Even if we run the risk of sinking our own exhibition, so be it. But we will have done our duty."

The group looked at one another uneasily and begrudgingly passed on to the next room. "How can I thank you, Herr Klimt?"

"Pass it along to the next generation. That's how everything is repaid."

The Werkstätte published a fantasy called *The Dreaming Youths*. The slender book of verses was dedicated to Klimt "in deepest reverence." It was written and illustrated by Oskar Kokoschka.

.⁻.⁻.⁻.⁻.⁻.⁻.⁻.⁻.⁻.⁻.⁻.⁻.⁻.⁻.⁻.⁻.⁻.⁻.

The Motor Boat

Following the opening, we left for our summer refuge on the Attersee.

"We are spending the year on a carousel, metaphorically speaking," Pauline said as she taste-tested potato salad before packing it in a picnic basket for Heli and Klimt.

My life was spinning, too. The salon was busier than ever. I hired more seamstresses. And I moved into a large flat beyond the salon. All Mother said was, "Are you sure you want to do this, dear?" Which was Mother's way of saying, "Now people will really talk, you know."

I walked down to the dock. The morning was dazzling. "Do you know how Rilke would describe the lake this morning?" I asked Klimt. He was sitting in his new motor boat, confronting a motor with hiccups.

"I sense I am about to find out."

"He would call it a self-contained blue, a listening blue, a densely quilted blue, a wet dark blue, a juicy blue...."

"But could he make a motor work?"

"Here, I brought you coffee, heaped with whipped cream, the way like it."

"Good. You know, it makes me furious when I can't get simple things to work. I no longer have the patience I used to have."

"To be the master of a motor doesn't sound worth becoming angry about."

"Maybe it's age. Ever since the *Kunstschau*, I've been thinking. I don't believe the young painters understand me. I'm not sure I count for anything in their eyes. Of course, this always happens—the younger generation must break away from the older one. But it's happened to me sooner than I'd expected. Still, there's no point in grousing about it. The inevitable just *is*." Klimt handed me his coffee cup. "Glad the Turks did some good while they were here."

"Egon Schiele adores you. And that brash fellow, Kokoschka."

"Egon I love like a son. And Kokoschka amuses me. His stuff is savage, but it's certainly not boring. To be boring is one of the only sins. No, he's audacious. And dashing. He's shaved his head, just in case we hadn't noticed he's different. Kraus and Loos are already promoting him as though he were their champion greyhound. I expect they argue about who gets to hold the leash," Klimt moved from the bow of the boat to the stern.

"I thought standing up in a boat was a sin."

"It is. That's the other great sin. I got Schiele a job at the Werkstätte designing postcards. Czeschka now has arranged a similar job for Kokoschka. It's a humbling position for an *enfant terrible*," Klimt chuckled.

"People say Schiele is a Klimt imitator. Is that true?"

"No, he's very much his own man. His own boy. At the moment, he's going through his puberty crisis in public. But after he's explored his—give me one of your phrases."

"Autoerotic obsessions."

"Well, that invites an entertaining image. I'm about to throw this god-damn motor overboard!"

Klimt jerked the motor's rope to no avail. "Anyway, when Schiele is finished masturbating on canvas, I think he will reach a wider audience. Tortured self-portraits of a skinny boy, which bring the mutilations of war to mind, may not be welcome in the Rothchild's front parlor. And he is ambitious—he makes no secret of that.

"There is no logical reason why this motor is not working. He's brilliant, truly brilliant—at 18! We've agreed to trade drawings. Although what he wants with mine, I can't imagine. I told him, 'Why do you want these things? You draw better than I do!'"

Klimt gave a violent jerk to the rope, and suddenly the motor buzzed like a thousand angry hornets. The noise ripped through the early morning calm, leaving it in shreds.

"That is the most horrendous noise I've ever heard!"

"I can't hear you!"

Heli ran lightly onto the dock with the picnic basket. Gustav extended his hand, and helped our slim, lovely niece into the boat. They were talking happily through the sound of the motor. Waving and blowing kisses in my direction, they zoomed out onto the serene lake, and sped away. Water smacked against the little boat, leaving a fan of froth in its wake.

Now the lake is "full of revolt—blue, blue, blue..."

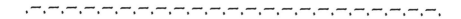

The Kiss

Oh, I forgot to tell you about the most popular painting at the Kunstschau. Klimt called it *The Kiss*. It was luminescent, sensual, hypnotic.

"You have more faith in the power of love now," Berta told Klimt. "This is the painting you will be remembered for. A century from now, people will say, 'Gustav Klimt? Ah yes, *The Kiss.* Trust my word." Berta and Hevesi sat in the Kunstschau café daily, trying to devise ways to combat the outrageous reviews. Today, Klimt had agreed to join them.

"I agree with Berta," Hevesi nodded. *The Kiss* is a sumptuous, intense, unified expression of love. Do we know the female model?"

"I don't lend my women, sir," Klimt said, lighting Hevesi's cigar.

"They are all in love with you. Surely you don't need more than a few dozen at a time," Hevesi puffed rhythmically.

"Gentlemen, this conversation is about to muddy the hem of my skirt. Your models are notoriously devoted to you, Gustav. All Vienna knows that."

"They come, they go. So must I. I find no pleasure being here. I feel like a laboratory specimen. 'The Artist The Press Loves To Hate.' If you solve my problems, let me know."

In a rare act of intelligence and official acclaim, the Austrian nation purchased *The Kiss* before the close of the show. The City of Vienna bought *The Portrait of Emilie Flöge.* And Klimt bought Heli a bicycle.

Gerstl

Early one morning in the fall, Rosi knocked on my bedroom door. "Herr Klimt is here. He looks sick." Klimt stood leaning against a chair in the kitchen. His face was ashen and when he spoke, his voice trembled.

"I don't know why this should bother me so. They do it all the time."

"Do what? Who?"

"Kill themselves. They kill themselves."

"Good heavens, sit down. Tell me."

"Got any brandy?"

"Rosi, bring some brandy. Who is it this time?"

"Richard Gerstl. Barely 25, I think. He hung himself. He also stuck a butcher knife in his stomach, apparently."

"How awful! Why does his name sound familiar?"

"He's a fascinating painter. Probably the most avant-garde of the new Expressionists. A friend of Arnold Schönberg. Very much the loner. He prefers musicians to artists." Klimt ran his hand through his hair. "I'm still using the present tense. Just leave the bottle on the table, Rosi."

"But why did he kill himself? Does anyone know?"

"You've been working too hard. You've neglected your gossip. During the past couple of years, Gerstl has lived, off and on, with the Schönbergs. Schönberg even took painting instruction from Gerstl. As a painter, Schönberg has this primitive, very frontal attack. Gerstl's influence, no doubt. Gerstl remained reclusive, had a hard time communicating. Except with a brush in his hand. He saw his subjects all the way to their bone marrow."

"I'm going to make you breakfast."

"It's not clear when he became infatuated with Mathilde Schönberg."

"Arnold's wife? She's the dumpiest woman in Vienna."

"To you, perhaps. Not to a lonely boy who was included in her household like a son. Or a lover, most likely. Apparently Mathidle ran away with the boy but returned because Mahler and some other Schönberg friends persuaded her that she could not leave her brilliant husband. For art's sake, you know. Apparently Gerstl couldn't bear the rejection.

"This morning, he was found in his studio, naked, swinging from a rope, a knife plunged in all the way to the handle. The strength that must have taken…"

Klimt poured himself another snifter of brandy. "What a talent. Gone. My father used to say: Life is like a chicken coop ladder—short and shitty. Little folk wisdom from Bohemia."

"I seem to remember a self-portrait. Laughing. Lit from below. Very strange and rather frightening."

"He might have exceeded Kokoschka, eventually. We'll never know. This I do know: He was afraid of nothing on canvas. Only in life."

"What about the Schönbergs?"

"They're not seeing anyone. Hermann Bahr called me this morning to tell me about Gerstl. What's happening to our world? There's a mounting sense of unrest. Almost a feeling of dementia in the air. Emilie, I'm sorry, I can't eat."

"What can I do for you?"

"Nothing. I need to get back to work." He took a final gulp of brandy.

"Will you be all right?"

"Yes, of course. As long as I can paint, I'll hang onto this life as long as possible. By the way, I'm waist-deep in kittens again."

"I think what you need is a docile 16-year-old dog."

"I think what I need is a wild 34-year-old woman." Klimt kissed my forehead. "I'll never understand suicide."

"Nor will I."

Bitte rubbed against our legs as we clung to one another in silent embrace.

Sonia's Visit

Eduard Wimmer-Wisgrill and I were having tea in my flat. He leaned forward, his teacup arrested half-way to his lips. "Join us, Fraulein Flöge. You are a superb businesswoman. We need you. You can create your own fashion department at the Werkstätte. Your sisters can run the Schwestern Flöge. And you can still oversee the place. We'll grant you leave whenever you wish. It's only natural for the Werkstätte to include a fashion department, and you're the logical one to run it. Do think about it!"

An urgent knock on the door: A frazzled Anya opened the door just wide enough for her head. "Fraulein Emilie, Frau Knips is here, and we're not ready for her. We're working as fast as we can."

"How much longer?"

"About an hour, I think."

"Don't rush. Quality takes time. Tell Rosi to serve Frau Knips a glass of champagne. I'll be right there."

"We're down to the last bottle of emergency champagne."

"Thank you. I'll order more." Anya retracted her head and closed the door. I turned to Wimmer-Wisgrill and took his cup. "As you can see, I have more than enough to keep me stimulated and busy here. But that's not the point. The point is: I love this place. I'll never leave it. You flatter me but I don't even need to think about your offer. My sisters and I are bound to the Schwestern Flöge. And to each other." I smiled, stood, extended my hand.

Wimmer-Wisgrill kissed my hand and sighed. "It's that kind of loyalty I want at the Werkstätte. I hope you'll pardon me, Fraulein, but you could use a decorator." He glanced about the flat with a pained expression.

"You are quite right. You can't hire me but may I hire you?"

"I would rejoice. Our best customers are the industrialists with their time and money. Our next best customers are the artists themselves. They haven't as much money but they have taste. Fortunately, you have both. It will be a pleasure." This time he kissed me on both cheeks. "I shall return with my tape measure."

I glanced into the reception room. Sonia Knips was delicately sipping her champagne. Klimt painted Sonia Knips' portrait in 1898. Berta called it "a breakthrough", a conscious move away from murals and theater curtains. Sonia's dusky pink dress, her milky complexion, her listening posture—the effect was lovely. The painting held your attention. Made you raise an eyebrow.

On the basis of this portrait, Sonia's society friends were eager to hang a Klimt likeness of themselves above their own fireplaces.

The triangular format on a square canvas foretold future compositions. When I first saw it, I noticed a small red notebook in Sonia's right hand. "Tell me why you're holding that little red notebook," I asked innocently.

"Klimt said I was too nervous. Well, I was. He has a very—well, it's an animal appeal, if you'll forgive my bold appraisal. I couldn't keep my hands still. He said I needed to hang onto something. So he handed me this little notebook."

"Um. I'm familiar with it. I gave it to him for his birthday."

"Oh, I didn't read it!"

"I doubt if you could. His handwriting is terrible," I said, as though confiding a secret.

That was 10 years ago. I remembered with a twinge of discomfort how jealous I once was of every woman who sat on the edge of her chair, squirming in Klimt's presence. I had learned to relax over the years.

Sonia Knips eyed herself critically in the floor length mirror as Anya administered tiny tugs to the skirt, minute pinches to the waist.

"I like it enormously, Emilie. You're a genius, really. Oh, speaking of geniuses, would you like to hear some gossip?"

"Only if it's about me."

"Well, only indirectly. My maid tells me that Gustav Klimt is being married. Don't you see him occasionally? I think I saw you two at the theater last season, didn't I?" Sonia casually watched me in the mirror.

"Yes, he's my niece's godfather as well as her uncle, you know. He's a good friend of the family." Years of restraint kept the tremble from my voice, but not the scarlet from my cheeks. So much for "relaxation over the years." Carefully, I placed the scissors on the table before they became a weapon.

"Well, it's only some little strumpet. I'm sure there's no need to marry her. My maid says she's a laundress. Next thing to street trash. She modeled for him, apparently."

"You modeled for him, too, as I recall."

"Well, yes, but he wasn't—"

"—interested... in you?"

Sonia turned and fixed me with a brilliant smile. "Do you suppose you could make me a cape to match the gown? In emerald green water silk, perhaps?"

I returned the smile. "Of course. Helene will be in touch when it's ready. Is that all?"

"That's enough, don't you think?"

As soon as she rustled out the door, I called Klimt.

"Sonia Knips was here. Her maid says you're marrying one of your models."

"No, no, I'm not marrying anyone. I could never give up our friendship, Emilie. That's all I have to say."

So! Someone wanted all of him! All or nothing. Is she a stronger person for choosing nothing than I am for settling for whatever is offered? Is this an important question? No! No, it's not!

"Heli's made a watercolor portrait of you."

"Is it any good?"

"She's given you a round stomach and a bald head."

"Splendid! A true eye. May I come 'round Sunday and see if it's for sale?"

"I'll tell her to double the price, now that I know there's a market. Yes, Gustav, come."

.⎺.⎺.⎺.⎺.⎺.⎺.⎺.⎺.⎺.⎺.⎺.⎺.⎺.⎺.⎺.⎺.⎺.⎺.⎺.

Kunstschau, 1909

Wearily, Klimt produced another Kunstschau during the summer of 1909. This show gathered the works of international artists: Van Gogh, Gauguin, Munch, Bonnard, Vuillard, Matisse.

Klimt added a new painting, *Judith II*. "The epitome of Jugendstil," Berta called it. And a painting that Fritz Wärndorfer bought years ago, and enshrined in his home. He kept it in an alcove behind locked doors. It was the 12-month-pregnant *Hope I*.

The day before the Kunstschau opened, Berta persuaded Klimt to join us for lunch. "You have no reputation as 'a starving painter' to maintain, so come enjoy a lovely meal," Berta coaxed.

Anyone as sensual as Klimt appreciated the color, texture, and smell, as well as the taste of food. "I judge a man by how much butter he slathers on his bread," Klimt admitted to Berta over *bauernsuppe und bier*.

"Speaking of the sensual—for a change—my libertine friend, surely you know that paintings of pregnant women make people very nervous. I am often asked why so many pregnant women are seen going in and coming out of your atelier, Gustav. What shall I say?" Delicately, Berta tore apart her roll.

"Tell them I am painting a series of stomach miniatures," Klimt replied calmly between slurps of soup. "On one future mother, I've done a very decent representation of the summer palace. On another, the Karlsplatz train station. Right now I'm working on Hermesvilla. The woman is expecting twins so it gives me room for the deer park, too."

"You would never lie to me, would you Gustav?"

"Of course not. I only lie to people who believe me" Klimt waved at the waiter. "Herr Uber! More beer!"

In the painting called *Judith*, Ricard Strauss saw "much of my own music, especially *Salomé*." In 1905 the Viennese censor forbade Strauss' *Salomé* from being performed at the Court Opera. Mahler was livid. "If an artist is not careful, he can drown in a sea of anger," Klimt told the furious Mahler. "We have to be able to float on our backs from time to time. Conserve our strength for the important races."

"And do you take your own advice?" Mahler asked.

"Does anyone ever take his own advice? I didn't know that's what one's own advice was for."

Klimt invited the 19-year-old Schiele to exhibit three portraits at the Kunstschau. The paintings were modern, but within sanctioned perimeters. They created no stir at all, compared with rumors about Kokoschka's one-act play, *Murder, Hope of Women*.

"That is the most insulting title I've ever heard!" Pauline gasped in horror. "When is it being performed?" she asked enthusiastically.

The performance was scheduled for the outdoor theater on 4 July. Kokoschka's poster advertising the play depicted a blood-red man lying in the lap of a chalk white, haggard woman.

"I marvel!" Berta exclaimed. "It's the most savage, the ugliest poster I've ever seen. I hear the play deals with a woman holding a man hostage in a cage. He breaks free and kills her. There's a rape as well as murder. Not exactly what an audience is accustomed to seeing while sipping lemonade in the garden. Everyone I know is horrified. Therefore, expect a sold-out performance. Trust me."

Berta was right. Before the performance, people craned their necks to see who else was there, as though they'd come to witness a public hanging. Tension knotted the air. People exchanged smug glances as if to say, "Well, *I'm* brave enough to be here!"

Klimt sat with Helene, Pauline and me. Heli was not permitted to come. "It's not a play for a young lady," Helene explained.

"But how will I ever learn anything if I am not exposed to life?" This was Heli's favorite theme these days.

"You don't have to know everything about life at age 17." This was Helene's favorite response.

Pauline and Helene fanned themselves and eyed everyone suspiciously. Klimt waved his cigar at other artists, nodded to past clients, lifted several steins of beer.

"I hope this won't be embarrassing," I whispered.

"I hope it won't be sophomoric," Klimt said.

"I hope Heli won't sulk all afternoon," Helene sighed.

"I hope there isn't a riot. All I have to protect myself is my parasol," Pauline fretted.

"Your parasol was an effective weapon last year, my assertive sister-in-law," Klimt remarked. "Ludwig Hevesi has a permanent dent in his ribs where you poked him at the opening."

Loos and Kraus scurried about like maiden aunts at a church social. Suddenly, a man screamed and rolled onto the stage. *Murder, Hope of Women* had begun.

A unified gasp was the next sound heard that afternoon. All the actors' and actresses' bodies were painted. They wore almost no costumes but their skin looked as though it had been flayed in order to expose their muscles, nerves, tendons. The result was moving pulp, raw meat reciting lines.

The plot, if indeed one could credit the play with a plot, told us that violence was inevitable. But the violence was very specific: Men against women, women against men.

Audience response varied: A few left, eyes downcast. A few snickered. Some determined that the 23-year-old playwright was earnest, and deserved their attention, if not their praise. Some were stunned and confused. And clearly some dismissed the play altogether and were content to watch the bodies gyrate and writhe on stage. I enjoyed the audience far more than the play.

At the end of the 45-minute tirade, the actors and Kokoschka walked on stage for their curtain call. Silence. The absolute rejection. Years later, Kokoschka would call this moment "a riot" and swear that Loos and Kraus alerted the police who rescued him from physical harm. But no. One by one, the audience filed out of the theater as though each of them had just remembered an important errand. I turned to Klimt. "Well?"

"He's pushing against the walls. Don't dismiss him. Now let's eat. All this raw meat has given me an appetite."

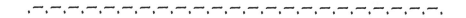

Vali

One morning when I went down to the street level to unlock the door, I found a young woman huddled on the doorstep wrapped in a blanket. She was thin and pale and couldn't have been more than 15.

"Oh, my dear, what are you doing here?"

"Are you Fraulein Emilie Flöge?"

"Yes."

"Frieda said you'd help me."

In the shabby blanket, she resembled a bundle of rags. "Come upstairs." The girl scrambled to her feet and eagerly followed me up the stairs, through the salon and into my flat.

"Rosi, make a good breakfast for our guest. May I take your—"

"Blanket. It's a blanket."

"Yes."

Beneath the blanket was a stooped, slender girl with strong hands. Not attractive. Not unattractive. And not at all like Heli. I was at a loss.

"How is Frieda?"

"Fine. Her mother says thanks for the cloth."

"And the children?"

"The two big ones are fine. The little one died of consumption."

"Oh, I'm so sorry. How... how do you know Frieda?" The girl's eyes told me I had asked an indiscreet question. "Through mutual friends? That's so often how it happens in Vienna. Would you like your milk warmed?"

"That would be nice. Frieda would've come with me, but she's working as much as she can to pay doctors' bills." The girl lowered her head over her eggs. Rosi and I exchanged glances.

I sat across from her and watched her devour her food. She ate the way Klimt did when he was angry.

"What is your name, dear?"

"Valerie Neuzil."

"And how old are you?"

She stopped eating and raised huge brown eyes.

"It's all right, Valerie, I'm not going to report you to anyone." At the same time, I wondered if I were already doing something illegal. Berta was better at this sort of thing than I was.

Rosi placed two more rolls on the girl's plate. "Good appetite," Rosi remarked.

I heard the women arriving in the cutting room. "Valerie, I must leave. I think you should let Rosi draw you a bath and give you a nightgown and put you to bed. You spent the night in the doorway, didn't you?"

"Yes, Fraulein."

"I'll come see you later. Don't worry about anything right now. You'll be safe here." Rosi raised an eyebrow. I sensed what she was thinking: What if the child has run away from home, and her parents are frantic? What if she has some dreadful contagious disease? And I was thinking: What if she's a thief, and tomorrow all my jewelry has vanished, along with this cleaned-up, well-fed waif?

My morning was too busy to call Berta. Helene was upset because the superb Minerva Roller missed her appointment to discuss her fall wardrobe. Pauline was upset because Fritzi Maria-Beer had dropped by to smoke a cigar, thus offending several customers. And Anya was upset because she is convinced that the new bolts of silk from Paris are inferior to last year's order.

When I returned to the flat in the afternoon, Valerie was sitting at my dressing table, staring at her reflection in the mirror. I sat on the bed. "Would you like to tell me something about yourself?" I tried not to sound judgmental.

She watched me in the mirror. "Why are you being so nice to me?"

"Well… I don't know why you were shivering on my doorstep, but I expect you have a good reason. I have a niece who is very dear to me. If she were, for whatever reason, discovered on a doorstep, I hope someone would be kind to her."

"That's all you want? You just want to be *kind* to me?" The girl's brow wrinkled, her thin arms hugged her body.

"Valerie, what did Frieda tell you about me and how did you find me? What sort of expectations did you come here with?"

The child sat down on the dressing table bench and looked at her hands, knotted in her lap. "Frieda said I could trust you. We work together, sort of. Except… I don't much like the work."

"You're very young to be a lady of the evening," I said gently.

"How do you know that's what I am?"

"It's just a guess. You're very aggressive for a youngster without visible parents or visible income. And you're no stranger to sadness or hunger. You've shown me that already."

The hostility in her voice lessened. "Frieda said you're not like the others. I'm sort of without a place to stay."

"Where are your parents?"

"My mother went to Linz a long time ago. I don't think she's coming back. I don't know where my father is. Italy, maybe."

"And you've been on your own since your Mother left?"

"I've had friends. Sometimes."

"And now?"

"Some of the girls say they get used to being beaten. I don't think I ever will. I ran away. Frieda didn't have room for me. All she could think of was coming here. He won't ever find me here." Valerie's gaze wandered around the room. "I've never been in a place like this. Do you think I could have more to eat? Please?"

"Not only that, let's find you something to wear. My niece often stays here. We'll find you something of hers."

Oh God, what on earth was I going to do with this sad youngster? She's not like one of Klimt's kittens, she couldn't just be given away, but I was not prepared to become an overnight parent to a child prostitute.

For the next few weeks, I employed her to sweep, empty wastebaskets and run errands in the salon. She watched the cutters carefully, did some basting for the seamstresses, asked intelligent questions and made a doll out of scraps. Rosi liked her.

"She's feeling better. Look at her, Fraulein."

From the window, we could see Valerie on the street, walking past the Casa Piccola's outdoor café. Several men let their glances linger on her firm young hips. "Rosi, do you think Valerie's attractive?"

Rosi frowned. "Get her to stand up."

The next morning, one of my models did not arrive for a showing. I told Helene, "Sophie is late for the last time."

"What are you going to do? Frau Primavesi is due in an hour."

"I have an idea. Valerie, come here, dear. We have a very important customer coming within the hour. I need someone to model for her. You're just about Sophie's size."

"Me? You're going to let me wear the dresses?"

"If you follow my instructions very carefully. First, you are proud of yourself and proud of our gowns, alright? So you stand with your chin raised and your chest raised. More. More. Good. Now, gently lower your shoulders. Yes. Now, bring your hips directly under your upper body—not too far forward, not too far back. There. Now. Walk."

"I can't. I'm paralyzed. If I move, I'll fall apart."

"No you won't. Try it."

The child looked like a porcelain doll come to life. At first, she was stiff and awkward. But after several minutes of strolling around the reception room, she began to smile. And her unhappy background, tawdry and unhealthy though it was, gave her sophistication beyond her years. Her youth and her experience was an intriguing combination.

"How do I look?"

"You look wonderful, doesn't she, Helene?" Helene thought my "adoption" of Valerie was one of my more demented decisions. Pauline, to my surprise, thought Valerie was a splendid addition to the salon. "Probably all she needs is some discipline and good food.

She should learn to play the piano. There's nothing like scales for discipline."

(Yesterday I asked Valerie, "Would you like to take piano instruction from Pauline?"

Valerie paled. "You're not going to make me, are you?"

"Not if you don't want to. My own piano career was dismal. After two years, all I could play were Luthern hymns."

"What's a Luthern?")

On this particular morning, a new Valerie was blossoming before our eyes. "I feel *elegant*. I've never felt elegant before! I bet the Empress doesn't feel as elegant as me!"

"That's exactly how I want you to feel. Frau Primavesi must believe that she is not just buying beautiful gowns, she is buying the elegant feeling that comes from wearing the gowns. Do you understand?"

"All I have to do is walk around? I don't have to talk, do I?"

"No!" Helene answered sharply, then smiled. "Shall we use a little makeup? Just a touch of color?"

"I used to wear makeup all the time!"

"Not that kind of makeup," Helene said grimly. "Come with me."

Eugenia Primavesi draped her furs over a chair and accepted a glass of champagne. "Emilie, it's too early in the morning. I feel absolutely wicked! You don't know how excited I am to be choosing my own clothes. Otto always made these decisions on my behalf. I'm so relieved that Herr Klimt talked him into allowing me to decide what I want to wear. It's really quite an adventure!"

"Would you show Frau Primavesi the first gown, please?" I asked the mirrored wall. From behind the partition emerged an exquisite young woman, walking smoothly, holding her head as though she wore a crown. The gown had never looked so regal.

After an hour, Frau Primavesi was delighted, the salon was many thousands of kronen richer and our Valerie had begun a new life. As Eugenia Primavesi was leaving, she pressed a generous tip into Valerie's hand. "You're new here, aren't you? What's your name?"

Without blinking, Valerie said, "Vali. My name is Vali."

"Lovely child. Class does tell."

After Frau Primavesi left, I turned to our little model. "Vali?"

"Yes. That's who I'm going to be from now on."

"A very nice name. Now let's remove the makeup and sweep the floor."

Music from the Ballroom

Klimt had been in Paris, Prague, Munich, Venice and Berlin, overseeing the installation of his paintings in exhibitions, and receiving honors everywhere. In Vienna, he continued to paint wealthy women. These women paid him handsomely. He, in turn, paid his models handsomely. As Heli recognized, Klimt was attracted to all women; each possessed some quality that fascinated him.

So when Klimt met Vali, I was not surprised that his eyes burned and his movements became liquid and deliberate.

"I want her to sit for me."

"No."

"Why not?"

"She's still fragile. I don't want… complications."

"I rarely make promises, but I'll promise you this: I will not touch her. You have my word."

I knew he believed what he was saying now, at this moment, as we walked one bright Sunday morning along the Danube. But how did I know—how did *he* know— what might happen in his atelier when the light of a new woman shone before him, when it was so easy to let his smock drop to the floor, and tenderly explore a hurt and vulnerable body that perhaps had never known a lover as gentle as Klimt would be with this damaged girl?

"Emilie, I take enough advantage of your grace. I will not betray you with this girl. I will treat her as a second Heli."

We walked in silence. "I don't know."

"I hope you decide to let her sit for me. It's your decision."

"And hers."

"Of course."

Several weeks later, I dropped off a new smock for Klimt. Everyone thought he owned one but he had many. They became paint-smeared, he spilled food on them, he caught them on underbrush. This is not a careful man—except with a paintbrush in hand or a woman in bed.

Vali was with me. We were returning from Mother's where Vali and Heli tried to find a common subject for conversation over tea, to little avail. Heli was hurt that another young woman had entered my life.

Mother had no idea that Vali's past was "stained," to quote Pauline. My sisters and I had decided not to tell Mother how Vali came to be living at my flat. We told Mother that Vali was an orphan and that her aunt had asked us to apprentice her at the salon. "This is not a lie, it's a fantasy fabrication," Pauline remarked approvingly.

When Vali and I arrived, Klimt looked gleeful. "Perfect! I have someone I want you both to meet."

He led us into his small, sunny kitchen. Sitting on the window sill was a wisp of a young man with a shock of wild hair and luminous eyes. He was properly dressed in a suit with a starched collar. His hands were jammed into his pockets.

"Fraulein Emilie Flöge and Fraulein Valerie Neuzil, may I present Herr Egon Schiele. Now let's drop the formalities and have some new wine."

Egon Schiele kissed my hand, raised his head and studied my face. "It pleases me to meet you at last," he said politely. What I felt he said was, "Take off your clothes." No wonder he and Klimt were so compatible.

Then he looked at Vali and the room crackled. I glanced at Klimt to see if we had become, in this one instant, the "older generation." But the voyeur in Klimt was reveling in the electricity tingling around us. Schiele bent over Vali's hand and she almost fainted.

The rest of the visit was ridiculous. Klimt grinned, cut huge slabs of bread and cheese and watched Egon Schiele and Vali Neuzil fall in love. I made inconsequential conversation and felt as though I were looking through a keyhole.

Within a week, Vali had packed a tiny bag and announced, "Emilie, I have to be with him. Nothing else matters. Nothing."

"Vali, listen. You have a new life here. A respectable life. I'm not saying don't become friends with Egon Schiele, but to live with him? My God, you barely know him. Yes, he is very handsome. And I know you feel a romantic pull. But believe me, that's not what love is—the sweating palms and the sick-to-your-stomach feeling and crying over nothing and not hearing anything anyone says to you…"

And then I heard the music… and saw Klimt across a ballroom. I stopped and looked at Vali, gasping for air in a familiar whirlpool of misery and ecstasy.

"Oh, Vali… I'll have Gunther take you in the carriage. My heart is with you."

She threw herself into my arms. "I knew you'd understand! Frieda was right, you *are* different. You're the best person I ever met! Thank you! Thank you!"

I knew exactly how she felt. And that's why my heart was breaking.

.⁻.

Gropius

Alma and Gustav Mahler spent "the music season" in New York City, but his contract permitted them to summer in Europe. Yet even during the "season", they were never far from Anna Schlinder Moll. When something went wrong, Anna Moll was sent for and with great dispatch, Alma's loyal mother sailed across the Atlantic to their side.

In January, 1910, Alma wrote asking me to find her a corset *"with truly marvelous uplift. Send it over with Mother on her next trip."* Her postscript was longer than the letter: *"I'm convinced Gustav is more comfortable with Mother and her husband than he is with me. And he doesn't lecture them, either. Perhaps I should have brought little Anna with me. He could lecture her to his heart's content, since he treats me as though I am his three-year-old daughter, and he treats her as though she is grown-up-wise and understands him. Still, I'm glad I left the child in Vienna with Mother. She would be constantly under foot at the hotel. Remember to look for sturdy stays of steel, not whalebone, as they are easily bent out of shape. Until our summer visit, I remain, Faithfully Yours, Alma."*

A month later, another note from New York, quintessential Alma: *"Dear Emilie, today I realized something very strange. I am not happy, I am not unhappy. I am living what only appears to be a life. I suffer, but I don't know why or what for. I am not free. I long for love or life or anything that can release me. My ship is in the harbor, but it has sprung a leak. Ask Pauline to send me a blue satin hat. Yours, Alma."*

Before she came to Vienna that summer, Alma spent six weeks at a spa in Tobelbad. Although she was in excellent health, Alma frequently "took the cure", along with many wealthy women whose complaints were diagnosed as "nerves." Aside from protecting Mahler from distractions and interruptions, Alma had little to do in New York. I suspected much of her general malaise was caused by boredom.

Following this latest cure, Alma sent me a note asking if we might have tea. I invited her to my flat which Eduard Wimmer-Wisgrill had decorated in silver and burgundy. It was both comfortable and modern. I loved it. "And not a peacock feather in sight," Klimt noted with approval.

I was curious to hear about New York, but as usual, Alma was at her best as narrator of her own life.

"Emilie, your flat is gorgeous! And this chocolate is divine. We couldn't eat chocolate at the spa. But this handsome young man sneaked me some. Oh, I must tell you about him! His name is Walter Gropius and he was a patient at the spa, too. We took long, sensual walks and he listened to all my dreams and frustrations. We talked for hours every day.

"Anyway, once I'd returned to Mahler in this little white farmhouse we're renting at Toblach, Walter sent him a letter, asking Mahler if he might marry me! Can you imagine? Well, Mahler was very curious. I can't say I blame him."

"Uh, yes, I think your husband's curiosity was appropriate."

"We tried to talk but we were both defensive. We needed someone to interpret us to ourselves. So we called Mother. She made me see that I could still be happy with Mahler. And she made Mahler see that he must treat me differently, if he didn't want to lose me."

Alma had eaten half a box of chocolates. She was having a marvelous time. "I think I've convinced Mahler that I need more attention paid to me. I've made him see that everything revolves around *his* needs, *his* work, *his* desires." She delicately licked melted chocolate from her fingers.

"He ignores all birthdays and anniversaries, as well as Christmas, even though he converted. Good heavens, Christmas is the best part about being a Christian! I told him he treats me like a secretary or a housekeeper. And the only time he comes to my room at night is after I'm fast asleep. That's not the way it's supposed to be, is it?"

"No, Alma, that is not the way it's supposed to be. Or so I've heard."

"Yes, of course, poor dear. That subject is outside your frame of reference. Now this is the amazing part: Mahler and I were driving in Toblach, when I saw Walter Gropius standing by a bridge. After we got home, I told Mahler."

"Why?"

"Well, I thought Walter might have come to abduct me. That happens, you know. Operas are filled with that sort of thing. So do you know what Mahler did?"

"I can't imagine," I said truthfully.

"He returned to town to find Walter! And when he did, he led him back home by lantern light. Well, you can imagine my surprise when Mahler entered, carrying the lantern, followed by a very nervous Walter. Then Mahler said, 'Make up your mind, once and for all, Alma. I will abide by your decision. I know it will be the right one,' and went to his room. Oh, Emilie, I hate that kind of responsibility!"

"Did you call your Mother?"

"No, there wasn't time! Walter was so persuasive. And he is brilliant, really. I forgot to tell you—he's an architect. You see, I'm not sure Mahler will ever be a truly famous composer. Not that that would make a difference, of course."

"Of course."

"But there is the child. And Mahler's madly in love with me. More than I am with him, I know. And when I thought about running away with Walter, I realized I just didn't have the courage. You have to practice courage little by little, don't you think?"

"So you and Gustav are reconciled?"

"Yes, I guess so. He was so upset, he went to see Dr. Freud in Leiden. They walked for hours along the canal. Dr. Freud said that I loved my father and I chose Mahler because he is so much older, and that Mahler is looking for his mother in every woman. Do you think that's true?"

"I have no idea. That's all he said?"

"Apparently. But Mahler felt better, so the walk did him good, anyway. Emilie, I must dash. Oh, listen to this! Mahler has now begun to leave little notes by my bedside. This is what was waiting for me last night…" She rummaged in her purse and found a paper, which she unfolded with great ceremony.

"'My darling, my lyre, come and exorcise the spirits of darkness. They claw hold of me, they throw me to the ground. Don't leave me, my staff, come soon, so that I can rise up. I lie and wait and ask in the silence of my heart whether I can still be saved or whether I am damned.' Isn't that sweet?"

I thought, "Yet another version of, 'Take off your clothes.'"

Alma stuffed the note back into her purse. "Oh! I almost forgot: The corset is agony but I look divine! And thank Pauline for the hat. I'll wear it in Munich. We're going to Munich for the premiere of Mahler's Eighth Symphony. He's dedicated it to me. Oh, Emilie, I hope I like it."

Alma managed to stand, kissed me on both cheeks, daintily plopped a final chocolate into her mouth and careened out the door.

"Rosi! There's not much to clean up. Take the extra chocolate to the women in the cutting room. I won't be needing chocolate again for a while."

.⌐.

The Eighth Symphony

Carl Moll reported to Klimt details of the Eighth Symphony premiere in Munich. All performances were sold out before the opening. The audience greeted Mahler with a standing ovation as he walked to the podium. He was more than usually nervous; he knew the work would excite passion either for or against.

Moll recalled "total silence throughout the symphony. Then, after the final note, the auditorium burst into one great cheer. The entire audience stormed the stage. Gustav and Alma were almost crushed. And then the parties! At one, Alma was offered a choice of gifts. She chose three baroque pearls on a gold chain. The hotel rooms were filled with roses, we could hardly find our beds. And Thomas Mann sent his latest book to the hotel. Called it 'a very poor return for what I received, a mere feather's weight in the hand of the man who expresses the art of our time in its profoundest and most sacred form. Perhaps it may afford you tolerable entertainment for an idle hour or two.' Imagine! Tolerable entertainment!"

The Molls were indeed pleased with their son-in-law. Moll found the Mahlers a house south of Vienna. After one more season in America, Gustav and Alma planned to reestablish themselves in Austria.

Suddenly, Fate, who seems jealous of too much happiness, intervened. Moll called Klimt to say that Anna Moll had been summoned to New York. Mahler was fatally ill, but determined to live long enough to die in Vienna. Moll was despondent.

He was with Gustav Mahler when the brilliant composer died. Alma was not. The bells pealed throughout Vienna a little after 11 on the evening of 18 May, 1911. Mahler was buried beside his daughter, Maria.

I sent Alma a large box of chocolates. I knew she'd understand.

.⁻.⁻.⁻.⁻.⁻.⁻.⁻.⁻.⁻.⁻.⁻.⁻.⁻.⁻.⁻.⁻.⁻.⁻.⁻.

Anywhere but Vienna

Everyone was restless. Artists were fleeing like hungry birds. They made their nests in Frankfurt, Berlin, Hamburg.

Some of our beloved friends were already dead. Olbrich, the Secession's young architect, died in Hesse after only a ten-day illness. The good Dr. Emil Zuckerkandl left dear Berta a widow. Handsome Max Kurtzweil committed suicide. And of course we still mourned Mahler. If I were asked to choose one last piece of music, I would choose the Ninth Symphony, written while Alma was immersed in mud baths, mineral waters, and Walter Gropius. Mahler's music is my "cure".

Josef Hoffmann designed Mahler's tombstone. "Mahler told me, 'I want nothing but my name. Those who seek me, know who I was; the others have no need to know.' So that is precisely what I did. He was, as usual, quite right. He felt estranged, right up until the end. 'I'm three times homeless,' he said. 'As a native of Bohemia in Austria, as an Austrian among the Germans and as a Jew throughout the world. Everywhere I am an intruder, never welcome.' But I wonder how his restlessness fed his creativity?" Hoffmann mused.

Hermann Bahr reported this conversation to me many months after Mahler died. Bahr had come to the salon with his wife, the opera singer, Anna von Mildenburg. Bahr and I were having coffee in my flat as she was being fitted. One of the benefits of running the Schwestern Flöge was entertaining certain husbands, while their wives were being tucked and pinched by Anya in a nearby dressing room.

Von Mildenburg was Mahler's mistress when they both worked at the Hamburg opera years ago. In fact, the singer claimed that Mahler jilted her when he met and immediately married the adorable Alma, so Von Mildenburg was not one of the late composer's worshipers.

"The pulse of the city is weak and erratic, Emilie," Bahr sighed. "When Hevesi killed himself last year, he knew something we are loathe to admit yet. Those who elect to remain either in Vienna or in life itself exhibit a fine, exalted species of patriotism. But when they realize that they are deprived of any opportunity to pursue their artistic aims because of the lack of sympathy or protection on the part of the educated—why, then, they are entitled to leave in search of a better homeland."

"Her-mann, come see meeee!" Von Mildenburg sang from her dressing room. "I am more beautiful than '*Sal-o-me*'!"

"Coming, my love!" Bahr called. He sipped the last of his coffee, handed me his cup and whispered, "Never marry an opera singer, Emilie. They sound so much better *on* stage than *off*."

Klimt made no effort to organize another Kunstschau. He saw his close circle of friends but political discussions were no longer of interest. Finally, he'd finished supervising the Wiener Werkstätte's compilation of his complex mosaic panels for the Palais Stoclet.

"The Great Pyramids were child's play compared with the Palais Stoclet," Pauline observed. "I'd like to have a spool of thread for every time they changed their minds about a bathroom faucet in that place. Well, I certainly like my brother-in-law's dining room: Pretty trees, no unclothed bodies. One could actually dine in a room like that."

A gallery owner approached Klimt, simpering, wringing his hands and bobbing his head. "Would the much honored and venerable Herr Klimt be interested in exhibiting the mosaics in my modest gallery before they're shipped to the Palais in Brussels?"

Klimt did not even answer the man. He just kept painting until the "little weasel" as Klimt called him, realized that the most he could hope for was to back out the atelier door with his aforementioned head still attached to his shoulders.

Klimt gave an interview to Berta, which she published: *"When you all thought I had simply swallowed the insults, I swore then that I would never again exhibit in Vienna. This frieze, upon which I have expended years of effort, would become yet again the object of the crudest kind of attack.*

"It's not that I object to criticism. But criticism that impugns an artist's honor—that is the kind of criticism which has forced me to resolve: 'Anywhere but Vienna,' if I am to exhibit at all. This is for me the only dignified way to defend myself."

Critics turned to one another and cried, "Why, I had no idea he would take it personally!"

.⌐.⌐.⌐.⌐.⌐.⌐.⌐.⌐.⌐.⌐.⌐.⌐.⌐.⌐.⌐.⌐.⌐.⌐.

Krumau

Vali and Egon Schiele were engaged in the tempestuous first months of an affair which left both of them thinner, exhausted and barely able to walk.

"Surely you must get out of bed to eat sometime," I said, taking in at the waist a gown Vali was going to model for me.

"Oh, Egon paints all the time. He paints me, he paints himself, he draws me with other women, and he draws people fucking. He has clients who pay him to draw only people fucking."

"Vali, I must say, this seems—well—most extraordinary, to put it kindly. I'm not sure I need to know these things. I just want to hear that you are happy, and that he is kind to you, and that you're being cared for so that you'll stay healthy. Do you know what I'm saying?"

"You don't think I should get pregnant."

"Exactly, and please keep your voice down."

"Don't worry. I won't."

"One… cannot always be sure."

"Emilie, I have something to tell you."

"Oh, God!"

"No, no, relax. I won't be able to model anymore. We're moving to Egon's Mother's hometown. It's a sweet little old town on a river. Egon says it has gables and spires and towers and it's sleepy and no one will ever bother us there. He says he can paint from sunrise to sunset and I can garden and sit for him and we'll find a different way to make love every day. Doesn't that sound wonderful?"

"Take the dress off now and see that it's pressed properly. And Vali— "

"Yes, *Emilie?*"

"It does sound wonderful."

Eviction

Later that summer, as I was packing to visit several of the Eastern provinces to buy laces and embroidery, Rosi knocked on my bedroom door.

"The girl's back."

Vali burst into the room, hugged me heartily. "Oh, Emilie, I'm so glad you're here. People are so strange!"

"Sit down. Would you like some soup? Of course you would. Rosi, heat soup. Now tell me why you're here and who is so strange."

"I can't stay long. Egon is picking up art supplies—this nice Herr Roessler gives him money. I guess I'm naive."

"Vali, start at the beginning."

"Well, we found this lovely little cottage in Krumau. Two rooms with trees and bushes all around on a path to a school. Egon used to sit outside, and draw the little girls on their way to school, and then we got to know some of them, and they would come inside, and I'd break a pastry into little pieces, and we'd share it, and Egon would draw them some more."

"And?"

"Well, they always called me 'Frau Schiele,' and one day I said casually, 'No, my name is Fraulein Neuzil,' and never thought anything about it."

"It didn't occur to you that in this tiny community, living with a man to whom you're not married is probably considered a criminal act? I didn't think I had to tell you before you left, that you must pretend to be married to Egon."

"Like I said, I guess I'm naive. This is as married as I've ever been! I love Egon. That's all that should matter. It's all that matters to me."

"Oh, Vali, that exceeds naive. That's stupid, dear. There's so much we have no control over, I'm afraid. So what happened? Why don't you eat your soup? You can talk to me later."

"Talking never stopped her before," Rosi said.

"Rosi's right, I can always talk. Well, one of the girls told her mother that Egon and I weren't married and damned if four sets of parents—all these sour-faced old bitches and their drooling husbands—came marching into our yard almost in formation, like Army officers.

"Then the gang leader said that the town had decided we were undesirable. The best artist in the world—'undesirable'?! Christ! They should have fallen on their knees and begged us to stay, and they should have paid Egon thousands of kronen just to draw their bratty daughters. I was furious! So I said some things I guess I shouldn't. Egon thought I was wonderful. He said he bet those pig-faced people never heard some of the names I called them. But maybe it wasn't so smart, because they said they'd have us arrested if we weren't gone in 24 hours. So here we are. This is really good soup."

"What are your plans now?"

"Egon is visiting his Mother for a few days, and he wants to see Klimt, and ask Herr Roessler for more money, and then we're going to a place Egon knows about 20 miles from here, a place called Neulengbach. I don't care where we live as long as we sleep in the same bed."

"I hope this young man knows how fortunate he is to have found you." I actually envied her.

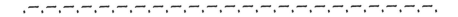

Discontent

I was invited to Loos' baptism with Kraus acting as godfather. I declined. I thought baptisms were for babies. Besides, I did not approve of these two grown men flirting with religion. Kraus was a Jew and should be happy to be one, I thought. I understood the sneer that accompanied the label: JEW. Being a Luthern who dealt almost exclusively with Jews in the shop did not endear me to Vienna's Roman Catholic power structure, either. But I had not been tempted to embrace hypocrisy. Kraus, however, had converted, and clasped hands with sincere Roman Catholics.

I found self-conscious Jews who pretended to be Christians a confusing concept. I mentioned my reservations once at lunch. Over a delicate *bienenstich*, Kraus blinked, fork aloft, "Surely you realize that being a Luthern—whatever that may entail—and being a Jew, is not an interchangeable argument."

Besides, I was staying close to the salon. I learned from Anya that someone in the cutting room was active in an anti-Semitic group. She frequently told the other employees that both "the poor Eastern Jews who don't know enough to stay where they belong, and the rich Vienna Jews who run everything" were responsible for all Austria's ills. The woman never expressed her opinions when I was in the room, but Anya reported that she was breeding discontent.

One day as I passed through the sewing room, I overheard one of the seamstresses saying, "I don't care how much money her customers got, they're still dirty Jews." Eyes raised and scissors stopped. Silence.

"Hannah. May I see you in my office." It was not a question. The woman trudged after me. I did not turn to see if she were looking defiant or frightened or embarrassed. I was writing a speech in my head as fast as I could.

I took my place behind the desk. I did not invite the woman to sit. "Hannah, what is your name?"

"You know it, Fraulein, it is Pitoniak. A Bohemian name."

"No, I mean your family name. Your father's name. I have it in my records, but I want you to tell me." I sounded serene, but I was sure the woman could hear my heart.

After a moment, she said flatly, "My father is Isaac Arnstein."

"Yes. Hannah, I read recently that the most damaging thing that can happen to Austria is when the Jews themselves become anti-Semitic. The writer said that self-hatred is considered Jewish patriotism. Now, I don't know what your story is. But you work in a shop where 90 percent of the customers are Jews. They are not only my customers, they are my friends. I do not need to be surrounded by people who hate my friends. Or themselves, by the way. You are dismissed. Helene will prepare an envelope with two weeks' pay."

The woman glowered at me, turned and stomped out of the room. Without giving myself time to discover how terrified I was, I walked to the doorway between the cutting room and the sewing room. Everyone was self-consciously very busy.

"If any of you are not comfortable with our customers, I invite you to leave. Our customers provide you with better incomes than you could earn at any similar shop in this city. Your personal feelings are your own. I have no right to ask anyone to change whatever she feels outside the Schwestern Flöge. But inside these walls, I will not tolerate prejudiced comments about our customers. For those of you who can abide by this rule, I will be raising your salaries next month."

One woman gathered her shawl and bag and walked in cold anger toward the door. All eyes followed her. Not a sound. Then the clock chimed, and broke the tension. I returned to my office, and sat numbly behind my desk for the rest of the afternoon.

"I don't know what to think, Emilie," Helene said unhappily. "What you offered the employees is money we don't necessarily have, and without consulting with us. It's very upsetting."

"I think what you've done is blackmail them. Can we endorse blackmail as a salon policy, I wonder? It's an interesting question," Pauline speculated.

"I'm sorry I didn't talk with you both. You weren't here and I just… did it. I wasn't thinking, I was feeling. But now that I *am* thinking, I don't know that I would have done anything differently. How would you have handled it?"

"I think I would have ignored it," Helene said.

"Do you teach Heli to ignore injustice, prejudice, cruelty?"

"No, but she isn't running a shop, either."

"You mean there's one code of conduct for Heli and another for us? Pauline, what would you have done?"

"Sicked Vali on her. No, in all honesty, I might just have asked Hannah to keep her opinions to herself. I am surprised, Emilie. I didn't think you were the rash type. Well, it's done now. How much 'be nice' money did you promise?"

"I wasn't specific."

"Good," Helene sighed in relief. "I'll have to study the books and see what I can arrange." She shook her head and opened the ledgers to begin finding a way out of the dilemma I'd created.

Pauline stood, walked 'round the table and placed her hand on my shoulder. "What you did was brave, Emilie. You followed your instincts. I know one person who would approve of that approach. Why don't you call him?"

Joan Kelley

The Fight

Klimt was supportive, in his way. "Now if Hannah and the other woman don't burn the place down, you'll know you did the right thing. Let's go to dinner. I took the liberty of asking Vali and Egon to meet us here at the salon. Cheer up. If you're going to order people around like a general, you may as well enjoy it. They seem to." Klimt sucked on a straw from Rosi's broom.

Suddenly—shouting on the street! Rosi opened the living room door abruptly. "Come!"

We rushed to the front windows of the salon. On the street, a heavy man in a bowler hat and overcoat was towering over Vali. I couldn't hear the argument, but Klimt didn't need to. In an instant, he was tearing down the stairs to the street. By the time I got there, the man was yelling at Klimt:

"The little slut owes me! I paid her for services not delivered. Get out of my way, mister, this has nothing to do with you!"

Vali was cringing against the wall of the Casa Piccola, passersby were transfixed, Gunther was working his way behind the man. Klimt said, with lethal calm, "She owes you nothing. Stand away, Gunther."

Klimt sunk into a wrestler's crouch and began a primitive dance. In a move too fast to see, Klimt grabbed the man's cane. The gesture was so fast, the man hadn't time to let go and went sprawling. Klimt threw the cane to Gunther and dragged the man to his feet. The man yelled vile curses, and tried to catch Klimt's smock. Oh, no, another ruined smock, I thought. But Klimt was focused and deadly. He hit the man in the stomach and face over and over until the man realized he was bleeding. With a final volley of curses, the large man staggered down the street.

156

Klimt stood in the middle of the sidewalk, swaying, panting, and sweating. "Inside, come, come," I urged. Klimt was very pleased with himself. His lip was bleeding but otherwise, he was still in one piece.

"Your hands. Are your hands all right?"

He held his hands out for me to see. "Best exercise I've had all week!"

Once we were upstairs, Egon Schiele arrived. "Egon, you missed it! You missed Klimt beating up Wilhelm—you know, the awful man I ran away from last year? Oh, he was wonderful!" Vali kissed Schiele's face and hair the entire time she was talking.

Klimt, still sweating and grinning, held a stein of beer in his hand, and a cold cloth to his lip. "Tell me, tell me," Egon said, fascinated. Vali threw herself onto his lap.

"Well! Wilhelm ran into Frieda and—"

"Gustav, this has been enough drama for one day," I shook my head, falling back into a chair.

Klimt set his beer on the table and squatted before me, grasping the arms of the chair. "We both acted today. Being an actor is much different from being a re-actor. You followed your conscience, I followed my instincts. We are both winners. Even if it appears that you lose sometimes when you let your heart and your stomach make your decisions—you haven't. You've won."

Klimt lifted his beer joyfully. "Congratulations!"

"I am so hungry, everybody!" Vali shouted. "Let's eat!"

.⎺.⎺.⎺.⎺.⎺.⎺.⎺.⎺.⎺.⎺.⎺.⎺.⎺.⎺.⎺.⎺.⎺.⎺.

Neulengbach

In April, Vali sent me a note. Could I send some fabric and might I like to see their cottage? She sounded homesick. I decided to make a day trip to their village. Klimt said, "Take the boy some oils. Here,'" and stuffed money in my hand.

"I don't know what to buy."

"Red, yellow and blue. Let him work it out."

So, armed with a large picnic basket, a satchel of fabric, and three huge tubes of paint, I boarded the train for Neulengbach.

The village was quaint and picturesque. I felt I'd stepped back in time. I asked directions to their cottage at the train station. The train official studied me a moment.

"Are you sure you want to go there, Fraulein?" I assured him I did. He shook his head, puffed on his pipe and told me the way.

The day was glorious. Their cottage door was open. Vali sat in the middle of the bed, darning socks. Schiele was cleaning brushes. The heavy smell of turpentine surrounded me. Vali looked up and shrieked. Schiele dropped his brushes in alarm. Vali threw her darning on the floor, hurled herself off the bed, and raced to the door.

"Emilie, oh, Emilie! I knew you'd come!" She caught me in a huge hug before I could drop my bundles.

Schiele donned his jacket and kissed my hand. The cottage was almost bare, except for a rough table and chairs, planks for dishes and folded clothing, books scattered about and an easel with a charcoal sketch of a young girl seated in a chair: A safe sketch. But tacked over the bed was a very direct, excruciatingly candid drawing of Vali.

"Oh, look, look what you brought!" Vali exclaimed. She lifted the fabric from the satchel, stroked it lovingly. "I can make the most wonderful skirts and curtains and pillows out of this. Egon loves stripes."

"Egon, I have something for you, too, courtesy of Herr Klimt." I passed him the huge tubes of paint. He took them, one at a time. They were size of—well, I had this extraordinary thought, and was instantly embarrassed. He continued to look at me, and I was convinced he had entered my mind.

"You're breathtaking, Fraulein. The color in your cheeks is most becoming."

"It must be the walk. Finding this place was an interesting challenge."

"Why hasn't Klimt painted you more often? Once hardly seems enough."

"Once was enough for me. Here, Vali, look inside the basket. Rosi bought all of this with you in mind."

"Ahhhh, tortes and jams and sausages and cheeses and a ham and sweets. We'll get so round we'll roll out of bed in the middle of the night!"

Schiele had not taken his eyes off me. "Emilie, perhaps you would do us a favor and sit for some quick sketches with Vali."

"Oh, that would be fun, Emilie! He works very fast!"

How could Vali be so naive? Her past life left scars that made me bleed with anger and sorrow. But now, this combination child/woman worshiped Egon Schiele as her king and her god. Her new-found innocence amazed me. Behind Schiele's eyes was a scene I did not dare think about.

"I did not suffer a drafty train ride and the stares of your fellow townsmen to model for artists newly fledged from Vienna. Let me wash up a bit and then I want to hear all about how you are and what you've been doing." I removed my hat and gave Egon Schiele my best "the subject is closed" look.

Vali managed to make coffee on a questionable stove. "Did you see the drawing of me over the bed? That's not really how I look but it's exactly the way I feel, sometimes."

"Yes, it's extraordinary."

"Oh, Emilie," Vali laughed, "that's the word you use when you're shocked. It's just a drawing."

"But it's so *private*. Hanging over the bed, anyone can see it, see *you*," I said uncomfortably. Vali and Egon exchanged a delighted glance.

"That is the point," Schiele said, sipping his coffee from a cracked cup.

Vali saw them first. "Egon?" she said quietly. "More company."

The knock on the doorjamb was not polite. Slowly, Egon placed the cracked cup in the saucer and stood with great formality. He walked to the door as though greeting Franz Joseph himself.

"Gentlemen?"

"Herr Schiele?" a short man barked.

"I am he."

"On behalf of the chief of police of the Town of Neulengbach, I have here a search warrant for this building." He tapped a rolled piece of paper on a tablet. The larger man behind him stared over his partner's shoulder as though he expected to find the room filled with naked women.

Schiele shrugged and stepped aside. I didn't know what to do. So I did nothing. Vali moved to Schiele's side, took his hand and glared at the officers.

The uniformed men stood in the middle of the room as though we were invisible. Their expressions said they smelled six-day-old dead fish. They moved in formation, as though to protect themselves against two frightened women and a slender boy. In the doorway to the bedroom, they spied the drawing over the bed. This was, apparently, what they had come to find. Together, they marched into the room. The smaller man ripped the drawing of Vali from the wall. His face colored as he studied it. He leered at Vali and sneered, "Is this you, Fraulein?"

"You needn't question the young lady. You may direct your comments to me, sir," Schiele said quietly.

"Young lady?" the man scoffed. The other officer was riffling through a pile of drawings on the floor with prurient enthusiasm.

I stood. The constable in charge looked surprised to see me. "Who are you?"

Schiele took one step forward. "Surely knowledge of the basic courtesies must extend as far as this village," he said with exaggerated courtliness.

"It's alright, Egon. Sir. It is my legal understanding that you must have a charge pending before you enter a man's home. Is this not so?"

"Oh, we got charges, alright, Fraulein. Seduction of a minor, dispensing pornographic material, eliciting minors for salacious purposes. It's all right here," he smiled slyly, patting the tablet. "A youngster spent the night here last week. You got a 'legal understanding' about that?"

I had no idea what Schiele's legal rights were. However, if I know this couple long enough, I'll become an expert on law, anatomy, street fighting and prostitution.

The officer in charge read some legal document while his partner twisted Schiele's arms behind his back and snapped on handcuffs. At the ominous sound of the metal click, Vali started to cry. I was afraid she might physically attack the officers or shout obscenities.

"Come, dear. Don't make matters more difficult." She came to me and hid her face against my neck. "I will see that appropriate people in very high places learn of this injustice," I said imperiously.

"Nobody in Vienna has say over what our judge does here, Fraulein. This pervert will rot first."

Schiele was in shock. His skin had turned gray. The chief officer rolled the confiscated drawings into a fat tube and tied them with coarse string.

"You're creasing the drawings!" Schiele yelled, agony swelling his voice.

The chief officer addressed me in the Viennese dialect. "This is an evil house. I don't know what your connection is to this pervert, but I advise you to take the girl and go back to Vienna or wherever you came from. You forget you were here and we'll forget you were here. A train leaves in an hour. You best be on it." The man tipped his hat to me with elaborate courtesy, and shoved Schiele out the door, and into a police wagon.

Vali exploded the moment they drove away. She kicked chairs, smashed china and finally threw herself on the bed and sobbed. "He didn't 'seduce' anyone! He's an artist! He needs people to draw! What's the difference if he draws an old house or a young girl? None! No difference!"

"Vali, gather your things and what's left of Schiele's drawings. You're coming back to Vienna with me."

"I can't. I can't leave him!"

"Next they'll arrest you for being an undesirable influence or something. We need advice and we won't find it here. Hurry."

On the train Vali sat with her mouth pressed into her fist and stared at the fresh April-green countryside streaking past. And I wondered about men who draw secrets for the world to see.

The Hermits

Every day, Vali sat for hours on the window seat in my flat, staring at life in the Casa Piccola café below. She was—by turns—furious, frightened, lonely, and depressed. She even lost her appetite. I forbade her to visit Schiele, fearing that she might also be arrested for lewd display or some such creative charge, since she was obviously the woman in many of Schiele's drawings.

Klimt called several lawyers. Yes, the Neulengbach judge was indeed the ruler of his tiny kingdom. However, the more serious charge—that of seducing a minor—was dropped. But too many people had seen the drawing above the bed, as well as many other equally explicit sketches. The pornography charge stood.

Art patron Heinrich Benesch kindly took watercolors and paper to Schiele in jail. While the police and various lawyers argued, Schiele was held in a basement cell. He was not offered any information about his immediate future. "He's not being badly treated," Benesch reported, "but he says he's wretched and there's no doubting that."

Of course, the melodramatic aspect of Schiele's personality luxuriated in the role of victim. But the imprisonment stretched on for three weeks without a trial. Even the most inventive narcissist would have been bored. Among the 13 watercolors Schiele painted while in jail, was a gray, crying self-portrait entitled *For My Art And My Loved Ones I Will Gladly Endure To The End*.

Finally, on the 24th day, a dour judge, representing the morals of the entire universe, convened a trial. Schiele was forced to stand in the middle of the courtroom while the judge delivered a scathing lecture against pornography in general, and Schiele in particular, and to make his point, he held the offending drawing over a candle flame.

"My father did the same thing years ago. I'd almost forgotten that," Schiele told us. "We lived above the train station in Tulln. My father died of syphilis. He was mad, of course, at the end. One night he went wild. I don't remember what upset him. He took all my drawings of trains and burned them. Burned them all.

"This was worse, I think. When you're a child and your parents are crazy, you don't know they're crazy. You think you've done something wrong. But this judge—he had a deep furrow between his brows—he isn't crazy, he just has no idea what art is. And he doesn't care. He was defending the world against this foul pestilence, this 'artist'!"

To an outsider, the four of us gathered in my flat presented the picture of a contented family. Vali sat on the floor with her head resting on Schiele's knee. I worked on a piece of embroidery.

Klimt spoke quietly to the head he was modeling in clay. "Put this whole experience behind you as fast as you can, my boy. Try to make peace with the fact that all artists are alone. We're hermits. There's nothing wrong with that. We need aloneness. No one can follow where we go. It's a sacred place."

Later that year, Schiele painted a double portrait of himself and Klimt. He called it *The Hermits*.

Assessment

Klimt painted another portrait of Adele Bloch-Bauer. This time, she was not buried in gold. She stood facing the viewer, her thin body standing at attention, her left hand clutching her coat. Klimt took the background from a Chinese vase I'd given him. "She looks on the edge of a nervous breakdown," I observed.

"Not everyone takes life's disappointments in stride as well as you do, Emilie," Klimt said. "I've known Adele for 12 years, painted her twice. She doesn't like either portrait." We were strolling through the Prater on a Sunday with Heli and Trude, my brother's daughter. We'd promised them an ice cream at the Lusthaus.

Klimt poked at the rushes beside the water with a long stick. "Adele needs something that absorbs her, something that requires focus."

"Her home is not her focus?"

Klimt was silent a moment. "Women as well as men need an interest outside their homes. The Schwestern Flöge is your focus. You've become one of the strongest women I know."

"You're right, I don't collapse with the first broken fingernail. But I work at being strong. I reshape my life again and again. At some point, I decided to live as fully as I know how without hurting those around me. I guess that's my philosophy."

We walked without speaking for a few minutes. The girls had found a swan nesting in the little river and were sneaking up on her along the bank.

"The butcher still asks Helene if I'm unmarried."

"I hope Helene makes it clear that every morsel of gossip is worth a pound of veal. What are you telling me, Emilie?"

"All I'm saying is that we make decisions, all of us, all the time. I'm happy with most of my decisions and the decisions of those around me. Not because they've been splendid, intelligent decisions, but because I've *elected* to be happy with them. Perhaps that's why I seem to have taken 'life's disappointments' in stride better than Frau Bloch-Bauer. It's been a conscious choice. Ahh, there goes the swan! She's angry! I wonder if she knows how beautiful she is?"

"I wonder if you do?"

"After all these years?"

"Because of all these years."

"The only thing better than sweet words is ice cream. Call the girls."

.⁻.⁻.⁻.⁻.⁻.⁻.⁻.⁻.⁻.⁻.⁻.⁻.⁻.⁻.⁻.⁻.⁻.⁻.⁻.

Alluring the Gods

Loos and Kraus continued to promote Oskar Kokoschka. "I even sold some of my Oriental carpets to send the boy to Switzerland," Loos bragged, using his most modest voice.

Recently, however, Kokoschka had fallen under the spell of the Widow Mahler, who had already managed two affairs since her husband's death. Or so Fritzi Maria Beer reported during one of her visits to the salon. Now Alma was rapturously in love with Oskar Kokoschka, according to Fritzi.

"Carl Moll instigated the entire affair. Imagine, throwing his step-daughter into the arena with that wild animal! Of course, any handsome man is a challenge to Alma. It's like waving a red flag before a bull. I saw a bullfight in Madrid once. Alma did come to mind." Fritzi blew a small smoke ring followed by a larger one. "I'm getting *good!*" she exclaimed.

I waved the smoke away. "Fritzi, you'll make the entire salon smell of cigar smoke."

"Don't deny me my favorite vice! Well, almost my favorite. To continue: Moll told Alma about 'this terribly talented genius. I should let him paint me, if I were you,' he said. I guess if he can't have an affair with her himself, at least he can choose those who do," she smiled wickedly and stood to leave.

"Fritzi! What an awful thing to say!" Pauline replied. "Shall I ring for tea? Surely you needn't rush off."

"How kind of you! So anyway, Moll invited Kokoschka to dinner. After the meal, Alma dragged Kokoschka to the piano, and played and sang Isolde's *liebestod*—'for you alone.' And then she asked him to paint her. I have it on the best authority that Kokoschka feels apprehensive: How could a man find happiness where another has so recently died? I think that's rather well phrased. Do you mind if I have another cigar?"

I ran into Alma several weeks later on the Mariahilferstrasse. She looked giddy with fulfillment. "Alma, you're radiant. How good to see you so happy. How is little Anna?"

"I put her in a school for talented children. I just didn't have enough time for myself with a child around. Oh, Emilie, I have the most delirious news! I am finally in love! Of course you've heard of him—Oskar Kokoschka. He's quite famous already. Remember how Mahler just worked and worked and didn't pay any attention to me? Well, Oskar dotes on me. Only that can be a problem, too. Here, let me read you this note he sent me today."

"Alma, really, it's none of my business."

"Emilie, you're my friend! Listen: '*Alma, I happened to pass your house at 10 o'clock last night and could have cried from anger because you continue to surround yourself with satellites and leave me on the dirty edge.*' Isn't that a marvelous image?"

"Alma, you needn't—"

"There's more, listen: '*Dear woman, do you know that I believe in you and trust in you and am rich as no other man? Be one with me forever, and irrevocably bound to me in eternal joy.*'"

Alma gazed at me with wonder. "I recall what my Father said when I was a very little girl. We were standing on the beach, and I remember the blue sky and the clouds. And he said: 'Play to allure the gods.' That is my destiny!"

And a glowing Alma floated down the street. Now it was my turn to gaze in wonder.

.–.–.–.–.–.–.–.–.–.–.–.–.–.–.–.–.–.–.–.

Different Worlds

Alma took seriously her mandate to lure the gods. She sported the young Kokoschka wherever she went. Eyes turned to stare as they shared her box at the opera to ignore Diaghilev's Ballets Russes: The strikingly handsome, endearingly awkward artist, and the flamboyantly stout, satisfied widow. Alma promised to build them a home at Semmering, on land bought years ago by Gustav Mahler. The ever-flexible Anna and Carl Moll, as well as Kokoschka, threw themselves into planning its execution.

Alma also promised to marry Kokoschka after he'd painted a masterpiece. That was the price tag for allowing the Widow Mahler to fulfill her role as muse. But Kokoschka was not yet recognized as the genius he claimed to be. One critic said his subjects, "Look as if they had experienced serious illness or several years in jail, as though they were suffering from repulsive physical and, of course, mental diseases."

The Emperor's nephew, unfortunately heir to the throne—should Franz Joseph ever die—was not a Kokoschka patron either. At a recent exhibition, Archduke Franz Ferdinand was heard to grind his teeth and mutter, "Someone should break every bone in that man's body."

So Alma was sharing her wealth and position with a painter many years her junior in return for steaming passion upon demand. (Apparently, when Alma shed the steel stays, Kokoschka was not too shocked to perform. "Oskar luxuriates in flesh," Alma told the horrified Helene one day at the salon while picking up her latest hat.)

Vali and her painter had recovered from his sojourn in jail and were settled into a good neighborhood in Vienna. Whenever I saw her, Vali's attention span lasted about two hours before she chafed openly for the insatiable Egon Schiele. "I had no idea pain could be so exquisite," Vali moaned, resting her head on her arms. I denied myself curiosity.

I continued to design clothing that released women from the bondage of corsets and fainting spells. I took Sunday morning walks with my painter. Lived with my guilt. Lived with my joy.

The three women devoted to the three outstanding artists of the day greeted each morning separately... and as one. Kokoschka might have been speaking about each of us when he told Alma, "Our heavens are the same but our worlds are vastly different."

.⌐.⌐.⌐.⌐.⌐.⌐.⌐.⌐.⌐.⌐.⌐.⌐.⌐.⌐.⌐.⌐.⌐.⌐.

Reflection

Otto Primavesi was a wealthy banker and financier who assumed financial responsibility for the Weiner Werkstätte when Fritz Wärndorfer finally spent his last kronen on the workshop. Wärndorfer's family shipped him off to America as punishment. But Primavesi was filled with faith and enthusiasm. He had purchased several of Klimt's paintings, and commissioned Klimt to paint his daughter and his wife. The portrait of the child Mäda Primavesi pleased Klimt greatly.

"She's already a great beauty. Sometimes I still think about..." Klimt's voice caught, and his eyes filled instantly with tears. He wiped his face with his sleeve.

"I know. Our child would have been five this year.… Please, we must change the subject."

Klimt swallowed several times. "I'm going to the Primavesi's in Monrovia for *Schweindlfest*. I'd like you to come with me. Helene and Heli, too, but they're primarily facade."

"Three extra people?"

"They have more than enough room. Hoffmann will be there. Others you know. Say you'll come."

"I'm not fond of barbeque, but I'm fond of you. If Pauline feels she can spare me at the salon, I'll come gladly."

"I've already asked her. You have her permission."

"You are a strange man, Gustav Klimt."

"What is it the Jews say? 'How is this night different from any other?'"

Flirtation

In early 1914, Schiele discovered two attractive middle-class sisters living across the street from his studio on the Hietzinger Hauptstrasse. One afternoon on the telephone, Klimt told me about Schiele's ingenious manner of meeting them.

"He made a series of semi-nude drawings of himself on banners and waved them out the window. Rather childish, but that's our Schiele. The women giggled and acted shocked, just the way proper bourgeois females are supposed to. He is now meeting them in the park, and takes them to the cinema with Vali."

"Well, what does Vali think about this behavior?"

"Schiele says she thinks it's another of his games. Schiele and Vali play games all the time. Childhood games, sex games. They're quite inventive."

"Oh God, she's so much in love with him, I expect she cannot imagine he'd ever become involved with another woman. Whatever goes on during the group modeling sessions I'd rather not imagine. But Vali is always included, so she's not threatened by those women."

"You feel very protective of her, don't you?"

"Yes."

"You're a good woman, Emilie."

"So is Vali, in her way. I don't want to see her hurt."

"They're both very young. There are bound to be mistakes. You can't live their lives. Come by tonight. I have a landscape I want to show you."

"I'm working late."

"Then come late."

"Will you feed me?"

"Now you sound like Vali. Of course."

I sat with the phone in my hand for a moment, thinking about the way Egon Schiele looked at me in Neulengbach.

The War Begins

On 28 June, 1914, the unpopular Archduke Franz Ferdinand and his wife Sophie were assassinated by a Serbian nationalist in Sarajevo.

When the news reached Vienna, people shook their heads and went about their business. At one dance hall, the music stopped, news of the Archduke's death was announced, the music commenced—and the dancers returned to their pleasures.

The decision to attack Serbia was motivated by the fear that the internal dissention which had been eating away at the country for decades, could only be stopped by a successful war against an external enemy. Danger from without would create unity from within.

At first, this seemed so. When war was declared six weeks later, Austria was overjoyed. Thousands of patriots sang in the streets throughout the night. Hermann Bahr became an enraged war propagandist. Several other writers joined the War Archives. Military units at the front were instructed to send the writers at the War Archives "three events worthy of glory" every day so they might create inspirational literary works.

Viennese men loved uniforms and they were indeed handsome in their military costumes, as I called them. There is nothing better than the rattle of a saber against his thigh to help a man swagger as though he has just won a duel.

Schiele was declared too frail to serve in the Army. But Kokoschka's mother and Loos traded one of Oskar's paintings for a horse, so that Oskar might be posted to one of the Crown's most prestigious regiments. His uniform was built by Loos' tailor and at 6'4", plus horse, Kokoschka was indeed an impressive figure.

At first, the war was only a slight inconvenience for Vienna. Alma found news of the war depressing, so she commissioned Pauline to make her a new hat.

"I'm quite bored by talk of wounded men and possible rationing." Alma sat in my flat, toying with her glass of absinthe. "I sometimes imagine that I caused this whole upheaval in order to experience some kind of awakening."

"Really, Alma, that's too arrogant, even for you!"

"Well, at least it's given Oskar something to do."

"Oh? Is he no longer in favor?"

"No. But he's still in my bed."

"Isn't that a contradiction?"

"Emilie, it's so confusing. He fills and destroys my life, both at the same time. He no longer fits into my plans. He made me lose my... *momentum*. He also made me pregnant."

"You're pregnant, Alma?"

"Not any more. We were at Semmering. I'm building a house there, you know. And Mahler's death mask arrived in the mail. Oskar hates it, he just hates it. But I *have* to have it with me, that's all there is to it! Well, Oskar and I had a terrible row and the next day I went to a clinic."

"Oh, Alma, *how could you?* He wants to *marry* you!"

"But I don't want to marry him! You can't imagine. Being with Kokoschka is like living inside a fiery furnace. It only looks beautiful from the outside."

"I'm sorry if I shouted at you. My nerves are sometimes on edge these days. This war is such a terrible thing."

"I try not to think about it. What I think is: I need a new man. Someone Aryan. Being the widow of a Jew, even a baptized Jew, is detrimental. Oh, other men are courting me, you know. A doctor and a conductor, to name two, but they're too possessive."

"How can they be 'too possessive' when you're still sleeping with Kokoschka?"

"They're all so jealous of one another."

"And you find that difficult to understand?"

"Oh, I understand it, but it gets in my way. You see, I want it all, Emilie: I want champagne and lobster dinners with the doctor; I want concerts and after-theater parties with the conductor; and I want sex with Kokoschka. What's wrong with that?"

"Even if there were nothing wrong with it, arranging your schedule must be quite complicated, and extremely time consuming. How is your daughter?"

"Fine. Berta knows everyone. I'm going to ask her if she can recommend a new man."

"How will you fit him in?"

"I'll get rid of the others. Kokoschka is the one I'll miss the most. But he is just too intense. He can make love for hours and hours at a time. I don't think that's normal, do you? Or don't you ever think about such things?"

"Intensity and artists are one word, I think. And now, I don't mean to be rude, but I'm showing Minerva Roller a gown this evening and I must see that it's ready."

"Kolo Moser designs for me, you know. Would you like to make me something?"

"Kolo is wonderful. I wouldn't dream of competing with him." I slid my arm through Alma's and walked her through the flat and the darkened salon to the stairs.

"Emilie?"

"Yes?"

"Are you happy?"

"I am who I am meant to be, I think."

"Emilie, that's cryptic! I didn't know you were the cryptic type!" She giggled all the way down the stairs.

Berta reminded Alma that Walter Gropius was once attentive. Alma traced Gropius to a hospital in Berlin.

Berta adjusted her reading glasses. "Emilie, the woman is quite extraordinary. She sent me this note: 'Walter fell in love with me in an hour. Perhaps I'll marry him. I would like once and for all to find my harbor.'"

"Berta," I moaned, "how could you do that to Walter Gropius?"

"Do you know him?"

"No. I know Alma!"

On 19 August, 1915, Alma Schlindler Mahler Gropius sent Berta another note: "Yesterday I was married. I have landed!"

"She makes herself sound like a beached whale." Berta sniffed the perfumed note. I had no interest in the beached bride. I was concerned about Vali.

Chaos

Schiele's "games" with the flirtatious Harms sisters had become earnest exercises in seduction, but with a difference: Schiele intended to marry one of them. And he invited Vali to choose his bride. Vali's response was to vomit, break china and flee their flat in hysterics.

By the time she stumbled into my flat, she was wet, grimy and wild with grief. "It's not true, it can't be true," she sobbed, sinking to the floor, her hands dead in her lap.

"Rosi, make hot chocolate." I sat next to her on the floor of the living room, my arm encircling her trembling shoulders.

"He painted us. I should have figured it out. *Death And The Maiden*. Egon holding me. I thought it was sad. But I didn't know it was his way of saying goodbye. Oh God, Emilie, what am I going to do? Edith's a piano playing virgin, and ugly Adele with her two-foot-long chin and loud cackle—I hate them both!"

Later that night, I called Klimt.

"Is something the matter? I'm working."

"Gustav, your young friend Schiele has gone mad! He's marrying one of the Harms sisters. You've got to do something!"

"Hmm. I suspect Egon's more conservative than we'd guessed. Vali was for fun, the Harms sisters are for marriage. Which one is it, do you know?"

"Egon explained it very carefully to Vali. He intends to share himself. And since Vali will remain his mistress, he asked her which sister she wanted to share him with. He actually thought he was being gracious. He's worked it all out: They'll be married on his parents' anniversary, June the seventeenth."

"There's history in that date. Schiele re-created his parents' wedding night with his sister Gerte on that date. Took her to the same hotel in Trieste."

"Good heavens! When?"

"When she was 12 and he was 16."

"How shocking!"

"It sounds as though Schiele has decided to become respectable, more or less."

"You don't sound very sympathetic. Vali's in agony."

"I do sympathize, I do. She doesn't like the idea of half the cake."

"No one wants just crumbs from the table. *That's a phrase I've lived with for a long time, Gustav!*"

"Emilie?"

"I'm sorry—but I'm very upset. Talk to him. Find out what's going on in that crazy head."

"I'll talk to him. But I won't interfere."

"I forgot to ask. How's your Mother?"

"Not well. She hasn't been out of bed all week. We take turns sitting with her. She doesn't always recognize us."

"I'm terribly sorry. I shouldn't burden you."

"It's all right. We'll talk soon. It's a strange time. Life feels surrounded by death."

.⌐.

Mother's Portrait

Within a month, Anna Klimt died, talking quietly and incoherently to her late husband as the slanting afternoon sun layered light on the patchwork quilt of her bed. Klimt came to see my Mother.

"Let me paint you, dear friend. It may ease the pain a little."

"Of course. I am flattered beyond measure. We can pretend I'm a rich woman and I've hired you for thousands of kronen. Emilie says you've just painted Charlotte Pulitzer. I'll be in very exclusive company."

So Mother went to Klimt's atelier several times a week and obediently sat without moving as he worked. The newest litter of kittens soon found a soft home on Mother's lap. Klimt's electric silence as he painted surprised Mother.

"My goodness, he doesn't speak! It's rather unnerving. But the kittens help."

One day, Mother came home carrying a fat kitten. "I've named her Palette. Don't you think that's clever?"

Mother enjoyed the kitten far more than the painting.

"I like to think something good is born of all experience," Klimt smiled, holding Palette over his head as the kitten chewed on his hand.

"I doubt Vali would agree," I sighed.

Confetti

Klimt did talk to Schiele. "What he wants is a bourgeois family life. It's my theory he needs to prove he can be the husband and father his own father was not. He doesn't see this kind of life with Vali. And Vali cannot conceive. Did you know that?"

"No."

"Injuries from her former profession."

"Oh God, I had no idea."

Schiele seemed truly not to understand why Vali and Edith—he'd chosen the prettier of the sisters—were both unwilling to sign a "contract" detailing how his time and energy were to be divided between them. Each woman would exercise her best skills on his behalf: One would create a proper home to satisfy his familial requirements and one would maintain wild and wanton ways to satisfy his sexual requirements.

For four years, Vali had defended Schiele, traveled with him from town to town and studio to studio, thrown herself with trust and abandon into his *menages*. Her proposed reward was three weeks in the summer, and every other Thursday for "erotic experimentation." Edith was invited to explore "intimate bliss."

Vali stared at the wrinkled hand-lettered "contract". She had folded and unfolded it dozens of times, reading it over and over, not believing the words.

Then she squeezed her eyes closed. "'Intimate bliss' to Edith Harms probably means sucking on a sausage while somebody watches. How can she ever fulfill Egon's fantasies? He wants things done for him that most women would never agree to do, let alone love doing. My life is over. I'm not being dramatic, Emilie. I really believe only a few women have known…"

"The white ecstasy?"

Vali looked at me and nodded. She now knew the answer to a question she'd never asked. "Yes. I wish I could be like Alma what's-her-name and toss men away like chicken bones. But I can't. He owns my body, he owns my soul. I don't belong to me anymore."

I lifted her chin, she opened her eyes and looked into mine. "Vali, perhaps you've been too dependent on his love. That happens. I know this won't comfort you, but there is only one person we can be sure we'll live with all our lives."

"Ourselves, you mean."

"Yes."

"You're right. It's no comfort."

Carefully, ritualistically, Vali tore the wrinkled paper into tiny pieces. "Confetti for their wedding," she said softly.

Signs Of the Times

The war was not the brief skirmish Austria had intended. We soon needed Germany to join us against the Serbs and Russians. Vienna's two most important institutions remained fairly unaffected, however: The coffeehouses and the theater.

Karl Kraus and I had found something to agree about again. The war appalled us both. In a brilliant piece of reporting, Kraus ran two items side by side in *Die Fackel*, without comment. One was a review of the new Kaiser Wilhelm Café. The other was a report from the front. Both ran on the same day in the Viennese press.

It was really one of those social events, one of those pretty, typically Viennese 'happenings' at which one so likes to be on the scene. In a pleasant and informal manner, the great Kaiser Wilhelm Café yesterday afternoon celebrated its opening.

"At six o'clock, we went into battle, in silence, no one speaking. The comrades who stood near each other shook one another's hand. A soldier sprang forward, was however at once thrown back, his whole chin, his mouth all shot away; while being bandaged, half his tongue fell out of his mouth."

The well-ventilated rooms, which take up the whole of the ground floor and mezzanine story, are particularly beautiful, with their imposing, subtly toned architecture, which is brought to life by the magnificent effects of lighting produced by the chandeliers.

"Then all hell broke loose. The enemy machine-guns opened fire. It was terrible. Our comrades were falling left and right, our lieutenant cried, 'I'm done for!' His arm and leg were shot away."

And the seats in the cozy corners are so warm, so intimate, after the wide, brightly lit spaces of the main rooms — a truly German spirit of homely comfort reigns. One is greeted by the painted portraits of our own Monarch and of the German Kaiser, decked with flowers. Even in these earnest times, this concern holds high the banner of commercial enterprise.

"I saw dead men with their heads blown off. But if the tempest of the battle was terrible, the icy silence afterwards was more terrible still. Next to me lay men and horses piled on top of one another."

On every side, lively activity. People point out to one another 'who's who': the actresses, with their circle of admirers, up above in the delightful balcony-salon; the artists, the civil servants, representatives of the diplomatic corps, officers and businessmen.

"My platoon consisted of two men, all that remained. The trenches around the guns, in particular, were full to the brim. The company re-assembled. The captain, the lieutenants and 41 men were missing. The colonel greeted us with the words, 'Good morning, Number One Battalion!' He tried to continue but could only stutter for tears."

People crowd into the writing room and the buffet, which makes a specialty of light, delicious snacks; the ladies tickle their palettes in the confiserie, while smaller groups of light-hearted gentlemen settle themselves comfortably in the bar.

"Then the General spoke. He said we had virtually annihilated an enemy eight times our strength, that our battalion would go down in history. Then he cheered us and the whole regiment stood and wept."

This magnificent café has brought a breath of modernity into the Viennese cafe-life. Business continues until late at night and when you leave the Kaiser Wilhelm Café, you know that you will come back again tomorrow and the next day and again and again.

"We withdrew and were given rations but nobody had any appetite. At half-past- three we buried the dead and at seven we retired to the batteries where we still are."

I lowered the paper and stared out the window at the contented patrons in the Casa Piccola below.

.⁻.⁻.⁻.⁻.⁻.⁻.⁻.⁻.⁻.⁻.⁻.⁻.⁻.⁻.⁻.⁻.⁻.⁻.⁻.

Vienna Patterns

The atmosphere in Vienna was surreal: A man on crutches, missing half a leg, his head swathed in bandages and a woman in a silk dress, her hat trailing feathers, talking on a street corner. A dog stops to bark… at him? At… her?

The Schwestern Flöge continued to prosper, despite the war. "It's our patriotic duty to keep our spirits up," Fritzi Maria Beer said staunchly. "New clothes are good for the morale."

Pauline suffered from a persistent cough so Heli came to work full-time. Pauline sat down at the piano each evening at seven, even if she didn't feel well enough to play.

"We're like an old married couple, this piano and I. We don't need to speak any more," Pauline said quietly.

Vali appeared, disappeared. She sometimes modeled for the Wiener Werkstätte, but she remained distracted, profoundly unhappy. Vali's life was a complete mystery to Heli. "Where does she go when she's not staying with you?" Heli asked.

"She has friends," was all I said.

When the Austrian Army became a bit more desperate, Schiele was finally drafted. "If Schiele looks good to them, they're down to frail men. Can old men be far behind? My thinning hair and wrinkled brow have been useful until now," Klimt joked at Schiele's wedding, "but wars become indiscriminate the longer they last."

Four days after his marriage to Edith Harms, Schiele reported to Prague for training. The new Frau Schiele followed him. Soon Schiele returned to Vienna where he dug trenches in the deer park at Lainz and guarded Russian prisoners. His commanding officers allowed him to paint, however.

"They've let the boy keep a woman and a paintbrush. The war can't be *too* bad," Klimt remarked, forcing a smile.

Vali followed Schiele's travels as a hawk follows a field mouse— from a great distance, but never losing sight of its prey. "I'll bet she keeps her clothes on even when they're fucking," Vali muttered. "He'll throw her out in a year. I won't even scrape her off the sidewalk and put her in an envelope."

"Vali, Vali," I sighed.

People were doing unlikely things: Schönberg wrote a patriotic war song. And unlikely things were being done to people: Kokoschka was shot in the head and bayoneted by Cossacks. Alma refused to visit him in the hospital. After surgery and recuperation, he returned to the front and was standing on a bridge when it blew up. "This is a very discouraging war," he told Loos.

Kokoschka moved to Dresden and commissioned a most peculiar work: A doll. Not a small cuddly child's toy, a life-sized doll that resembled Alma. He gave the seamstress very specific instructions: The mouth was to remain open, lined with real teeth. It was to have authentic hair, in all the places authentic hair grows, and it was to be anatomically correct. He called it The Silent Woman in contrast to its real life model. He took it everywhere. You can imagine the sensation: Tall, striking Oskar Kokoschka, leaning over at the opera to whisper endearments into the pink cloth ear of the vapidly grinning Almost-Alma.

One night during a raucous party, complete with a beautiful courtesan and many of Kokoschka's friends, the red wine-drenched doll was thrown off a balcony. She fell to her death in the courtyard below. The next morning, a postman discovered what appeared to be a blood-stained corpse, headless and wearing expensive Parisian lingerie. The police were called and Oskar, plus whoever he was sleeping with, were dragged out of bed to explain the decapitated body. Almost-Alma had served her purpose, however—whatever that may have been. Instead of a lavish Viennese funeral, Almost-Alma was carted away by the dustman.

In spite of the strangeness of the times, the pattern of my life with Klimt was comfortable. One Sunday, Klimt was too busy for our walk. I sat on a kitchen chair in the garden, embroidering yellow leaves on the shoulders of a smock while he crated a painting for an exhibition in Berlin. I looked up and saw the face I knew better than my own. Twenty-five years now.

I watched the man I loved pound nails into a crate. "You know, we've worked harder on this relationship than most people do on a marriage."

Klimt lowered his hammer and slowly removed a nail from his mouth. "And it's been worth every minute."

We both blushed.

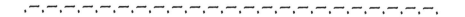

The Rich and the Poor

Horse sausage, dried fruits and vegetables, saccharine, cooking fat derived from petrol residue. Cornmeal bread, chicory and ground beets for coffee. Shoe soles of pressed cardboard and sawdust bonded with tar. Textiles of nettle fibers and paper.

And then there was Friederike Maria Beer.

Fritzi's clothes were designed and made exclusively by the Wiener Werkstätte. She liked my clothes, but she *loved* the workshop's clothes. And their furniture. And their jewelry. The workshop's items were costly and impractical. "Costly, impractical and mine," Fritzi gloated.

Schiele painted her in 1914. "I went to him not because I thought he was a great artist. What do I know about art? I hired him because I thought he was exciting. Very, very exciting," she breathed.

"I hope this isn't one of your lurid stories," Helene winced.

"Unfortunately not. The first thing he said was he didn't like my dress. Then he made me lie face down on a couch, and he tossed straw dolls all over me. Isn't that weird? I thought when he said he didn't like my dress that he'd ask me to take it off. I was prepared to do that! But I wasn't prepared to have these dolls draped all over me. And he stood the painting up so that I look like I'm doing a Spanish dance or something. Well, I've thought about it and I've decided that I should be painted again. Only this time by Klimt."

"I don't believe anyone has ever had her portrait done by both Schiele and Klimt. The contrast should be interesting," Helene said.

"It's a gift. I'm seeing someone who offered me a string of very precious pearls or my portrait by Klimt. I already have pearls."

Klimt's portrait of Fritzi was charming, I thought.

"I found it a little busy," Helene told Klimt.

"She has a 'busy' personality," Klimt replied. "Her jacket was so full of pattern, I finally asked her to wear it inside out. She kept saying, 'Talk to me!' I told her I didn't talk while I was working. 'But I'm so bored!' She must have said that six dozen times. Eventually, we worked it out."

"I don't want to hear about it, my dear brother-in-law."

"I didn't intend to tell you about it, my dear sister-in-law."

.⁻.⁻.⁻.⁻.⁻.⁻.⁻.⁻.⁻.⁻.⁻.⁻.⁻.⁻.⁻.⁻.⁻.⁻.⁻.

The Friends

One evening as I was locking the salon door, I saw a familiar figure striding briskly down Mariahilferstrasse.

"Vali, dear, you look wonderful!"

"I am. Well, a little wonderful, anyway. What do you have to eat?"

"Let's see what kitchen miracles Rosi can perform. Come."

After a mysterious meat and cabbage, Vali put her elbows on the table and proclaimed, "I have a surprise. I have a new friend. I saw Klimt this afternoon and I asked him if he'd like to paint us."

"He's wanted to paint you for some time. I'm sure he said yes."

"He did. He's always been so good to me. Like a father."

"I'm not sure that's how he sees himself, but I'm glad you're so comfortable with him. Now tell me about this new friend."

"We're so good for each other. I think I've found someone who really appreciates me for myself. Little by little, I'm starting to trust again. I hope it lasts a long, long time. Oh, look what time it is! We're going to the Prater amusement park. Doesn't that sound gay?"

"When do I get to meet your new friend?"

"After the painting's done." Vali sprang to her feet, hugged me, hugged Rosi and bolted for the door.

Klimt called one morning. "Vali and her lover are coming over tonight. The painting is finished. She wants you to see it."

"Are you pleased with it?"

"Yes, yes I am."

"Do you approve of her lover?"

"I do."

The painting is called *The Friends*. Vali, naked, looking sweet and innocent and at peace, rests her head on the shoulder of a woman in an orange robe. They are the picture of a happy couple. I have rarely been so shocked.

.⌐.⌐.⌐.⌐.⌐.⌐.⌐.⌐.⌐.⌐.⌐.⌐.⌐.⌐.⌐.⌐.⌐.

Partings

When Franz Joseph died in November, 1916, Vienna honored him with the usual pomp and circumstance: The fat, polished Imperial coach, the six stately black horses, their plumed headdresses trembling with every step. But the sidewalks were not overwhelmed with mourners as when Crown Prince Rudolph was carried through the streets by the same funeral coach in 1889.

Death was now a familiar figure stalking Vienna's streets. People didn't care that an ancient emperor had died—not when strong young men were being blown to bits every day. No, for the Emperor, there was little black crepe, few stores were closed, few tears were shed. Vendors hawked funeral souvenirs instead.

I closed the shop so that the employees could watch the funeral procession, knowing that they would use the time as a holiday instead. I didn't pay my respects to the Emperor either, although I was pleased to learn that Archduke Charles led Katarina Schratt to the bier so that she could lay two white roses on his breast. Quite a breach of royal etiquette. I took secret pleasure in that.

I didn't observe mourning rituals for a very good reason: I spent the day with Pauline. She had lost weight and her cough was much worse.

"She won't tell you, but she's coughing blood," Helene told me outside Pauline's bedroom.

"What does the doctor say?"

"Good food, clean air, rest."

"That's cheap advice for all of us. But doesn't he say anything useful? Can't he give her something?"

"I don't know, Emilie. You don't live here anymore. You're not as close to… things. You don't hear her cough in the middle of the night." Helene covered her mouth to hold back the sob.

"Shouldn't she be in the hospital?"

"She won't go."

I entered the darkened room and sat by the bed. Pauline, my wonderful, funny, sensible sister looked wan and tired. There was no light in her eye, no stubborn thrust to her chin.

"You're not out crying into a black handkerchief on the cold street? How can you resist?" she said slowly, with a wicked smile.

"How do you feel?"

"I doubt if I could carry my piano up a flight of stairs."

"Shouldn't you be in a sanatorium? We have the money, you know."

"Another week of memorizing the wallpaper in this room and I should be my stout, sweet self again." Then she grabbed a breath and coughed until her face turned purple.

The family met around the dining room table that evening. We decided the doctor should be told that Pauline was being moved to a sanatorium rather than wait for it to occur to him.

Pauline didn't want to leave the home she'd lived in for 50 years. But we thought the care would be somehow better.... You just don't know, do you?

Now we worried about her when none of us was with her, and we spent so much time traveling back and forth that we were all exhausted. I saw her less than Helene because someone had to run the shop. The house felt lopsided without Pauline. Pauline gave us balance.

The call came in the middle of the day. I saw Heli pick up the receiver. She looked at me, stricken.

Now we closed the shop. Now we attended a funeral. Now we grieved. We buried Pauline to Brahms, her hands resting on an exquisite gray satin hat with pearls and feathers. At one point in the funeral, I think Father put his arm around me.

In Mourning

Each of us returned to those activities that kept us sane: Mother canned quarts and quarts of strawberries and whatever else came in season—beans, tomatoes, beets. She made applesauce, applebutter, sauerkraut—whatever she could commandeer, considering the food shortage.

Helene worked out a more streamlined bookkeeping system for the salon. I learned how to make laces and appliqué and embroidery almost as expertly as old women in Romanian villages.

Sometimes, for minutes at a time, I forgot that Pauline would not be there when I returned. She would not look up, tap her thimble on the table and announce:

"Lace is nice if you have no imagination. Now velvet! There's a fabric with mystery, with soul!"

Heli, bless her, fell in love. Everyone approved: Professor Bloch's son, Florian. He looked like a healthy Vincent Van Gogh. Instead of sunflowers, he was devoted to banking.

"A financier in the family? Makes sense to me." I could hear Pauline's voice.

"Pauline, don't leave me! Join me! I know this sounds strange and we never talked about…. it, but sometimes with Gustav, when I am so full of him that my veins have to expand to make room, I feel I am him. I want your spirit to enter me. I want you to become us."

I sat on the window sill in the salon and sent these thoughts shooting into the turbulent sky. Clouds somersaulted across an amber moon.

"Now that's a seductive color. Probably thought up by my brother-in-law." Good. She's accepted my proposition.

Gladiolus And Sauerkraut

Klimt, the artist, continued to amaze. Berta saw it clearly: "He's still growing. And at the same time, those qualities that made him so endearing in the first place, endure. His message is Life. All the profound thinkers today—Von Hofmannsthal, Kraus, Rilke, Kafka, Musil—they are all deeply pessimistic. They view what may indeed be the last days of a crumbling world with cynicism and anguish. But Klimt! He gives birth—again and again—in a lost

Eden. His love for women, his identification with them, has been his salvation, I think. He is humanistic, he believes in nurture, in sensuality without shame. In this, he is very female. Did you take that down, by any chance? I am often wonderfully quotable!"

I laughed and hugged her. "And not only that, I agree with what you say. Thank you for tea. Vali is coming by. She has 'an announcement to make.'"

"Well, I doubt if she intends to tell you that she's being married in bridal white to her Lesbian lover."

"Berta, you make their arrangement sound seamy. Her friend is an interesting and intelligent person. She's educated, she's lived abroad—"

"Where?"

"Lesbos. Greece."

"That stands to reason."

Vali's arms were overflowing with gladiolus when she let the knocker crash against the door.

"Emilie! My dearest, my most best friend! I'm finally going to do something worthwhile with my life, a pinch of it, anyway. The rumor is that your Mother made applesauce and sauerkraut this year."

"I hear the hint. Set the table while I find vases for these miraculous flowers."

"Aren't they grand? I asked God to work overtime."

"I thought you might come by with... Vita, isn't it?"

"No, she's packing."

I looked up quickly. Vali was smiling.

"We've joined the Red Cross. We're going to bandage wounds and serve coffee all over the world. I'm not sure there is anything left for me in Vienna, except you." Vali placed the vase of gladiolus on the sideboard. She looked flushed with contentment.

"And Vita doesn't care where we are. We told the Red Cross we're sisters so they're letting us serve together. I really enjoy lying to people who make rules."

"Where will they send you?"

"I think Romania. The Romanians are always dancing and fighting. It should be fun. Well, maybe not fun, but at least we'll be together." Vali turned to face me, a napkin in each hand. "Emilie, you saved my life. When you found me on the doorstep. When the police broke into our house in Neulengbach. When Egon married the vestal virgin. You've shown me who I want to be."

"Thank you, Vali. Perhaps you've been the child I never had. Sorry there can't be sausage with the sauerkraut."

The Afternoon Fitting

Almost the last person I wanted to see was Alma, but she'd sent flowers when Pauline died, and then asked me to design a dress for her.

The dresses I designed were called "rational". They embraced the comfort of the grim "reform" dress, but they were also gracious, feminine, literate.

Heli was dressing one of the mannequins in the reception room. "How can a dress be 'literate'?" she asked.

"A 'literate' dress tells the public who the wearer is. It communicates a point of view, it says, 'My reason for being is to make you feel good.' Do you remember how it feels to float on your back in the Attersee with your eyes closed?"

"Yes. It's heavenly. It's rather how I feel when I dance with Florian."

"I'm glad. Well, that's how my dresses should make you feel. You've worn my clothes all your life, so you don't know what it was like—*is* like—for most women. They can't breathe, they can't move, they're enslaved. It's wicked! I want women to 'wear water' as much as possible."

"Frau Gropius is due any moment. Shall I prepare the absinthe?"

"You are wise beyond your years, Heli."

Alma was an hour late. She swooped in looking disheveled and sated. I knew the look.

"Oh, Emilie, I've just come from the Hotel Bristol. May I confide in you?"

"Wouldn't you rather just submit to your fitting and be on your way?"

"No! Coming here is better than a month at a spa. I'm sure you've heard of Franz Werfel, the poet and political activist? But ignore the political part. He's 27 and mad about me! We have this… spiritual link, so—"

"Alma, forgive me for interrupting you, but aren't you still married to Walter Gropius? Didn't you have a child last year?" I offered her the tray of absinthe, sugar and spoon.

"Oh, Emilie, you are so provincial. That's what endears you to me. If you'd ever had a torrid affair, you'd know how it feels to hunger after a man—no matter what the consequences! But alas, that doesn't seem to be in your stars, does it?" Alma smiled sympathetically, and waved the slotted spoon.

"Alma, don't spill your drink."

"Well! Franz and I cannot bear to be apart. Luckily, we don't have to be. He's in the Army but he's attached to the press office so he doesn't have to wear a uniform, and he's allowed to live at the Hotel Bristol. Sometimes the war is a bother, though. When he and Walter have leave at the same time, it's complicated. The baby isn't sure who her father is when they're both home."

"Who is?"

"Walter, of course! I hadn't even met Werfel yet."

"Forgive me. It's hard to tell the actors without a program."

"That is the ugliest thing you have ever said to me! I should take my business elsewhere! But your sister died and I feel sorry for you."

"Get out, Alma." I was murderously calm. Almost serene.

"Emilie, don't scold. I need your support."

"What you need is a serious spanking every day of your life." I was astonished by the sound of my voice: 30 years' of repression neatly expressed in one sentence.

"Emilie! You have just ruined our friendship! I have never erred! Surely you know that! For the first time in my life, I live with a full heart—and you don't care!"

"What happened to your plan to limit yourself to Aryan men?"

"Alright, Werfel is a short fat Jew with bulbous lips and watery eyes. But he has a brilliant mind. I was irresistibly drawn to his mind, and now I'm pregnant, and my life burns with anticipation again. He wants to marry me, of course."

Alma lifted the glass of absinthe, and smiled slyly at the memory of her afternoon at the Hotel Bristol. Then she remembered where she was.

"Emilie, I'm truly upset. You've spoiled my lovely day! I think you're jealous, that's why you refuse to rejoice in my happiness."

"Haven't you forgotten a detail, Alma? You have a husband."

"Who are you to even mention the word 'husband' to me, Emilie Flöge? You haven't landed even the first one! And you never will! Everybody knows Klimt sleeps with everyone *but* you!"

"I asked you to leave once, Alma. I would rather not ask again. I think I could throw you down the stairs quite easily, however, if you prefer."

Alma screamed, dropped her goblet onto the floor, sending the murky green liquid splashing, tore out of the salon and down the stairs, whimpering as she fled.

Immediately, I boxed the half-finished dress and sent it to Frieda's mother with a note: *This will look so much better on you than the person who ordered it.*

Then I called Klimt. "I've just been nastier to Alma than I've ever been to anyone in my life."

"Oh? How do you feel?"

"I… feel… wonderful!"

.⁻.

Oh, God…

I was signing checks late one night in the office. A furtive knock on the salon door below.

I looked out the window and saw Frieda standing on the doorstep, huddled in a gray shawl. By the time I opened the door, I knew something terrible had happened.

"What is it?"

"Vali's dead."

I don't remember falling, I don't remember being carried upstairs by Rosi and Gunther. I didn't want to regain consciousness ever again. They called Dr. Bauer. They called Klimt. Dr. Bauer gave me a sedative. Klimt held me throughout the night. Rosi sat in the kitchen, drinking brandy. Gunther sat by the stove that had cooked so many meals for Vali and wept openly.

When I let daylight in the next morning, Helene was sitting beside me. Klimt stood at the foot of the bed, looking wretched.

"Tell me."

"Scarlet fever. Vali and Vita, too. There was an epidemic, and the Red Cross sent them both to a hospital to nurse the sick and wounded. Vali listed Frieda and you as her next of kin."

"Where is she?"

"They buried her there."

"It's too much, too much…"

Klimt gathered me to his warm chest as though to pour his strength into my aching soul. "I know, I know," he murmured.

Helene stood. "I'll open the shop." In the doorway, she turned to look at us. "You two should…" Her voice trailed off. She bit her lower lip before continuing. "Life is so short. Ernst, Father, Pauline, Gustav's parents, and now Vali. I wasn't ready to let any of them go."

She closed the door quietly.

.⁻.⁻.⁻.⁻.⁻.⁻.⁻.⁻.⁻.⁻.⁻.⁻.⁻.⁻.⁻.⁻.⁻.⁻.⁻.

The Perfect Supper

On the snowy evening of 10 January, 1918, I was working late, hand-painting silk fabric for a pair of harem pants. I liked the silence in the cutting room at night. The only sound was Bitte's purring as she wove S's around my legs.

I looked up at the sound of footsteps in the anteroom. Someone with a key…

"Stick your needle in a pincushion. I'm taking you to dinner." Klimt swept in, snow reflecting tiny diamonds on his fur hat and beard, on the long blue cape he wore over his smock. He leaned on the doorframe, his eyes sharp and mischievous. "I'm the painter in the family, what are you doing?" he asked lightly. The word 'family' hung in the air.

Quickly, I wiped my brushes. "My vain customers will have to wait," I said.

"Good. I've always suspected you were corruptible. I'll fetch your cape. I want candlelight and wine and a long, hot meal in a quiet, dark restaurant," he shouted on his way to the armoire. "Georg told me about a little hidden place the war doesn't seem to have discovered yet."

He reappeared in the doorway and looked at me as he had the first night I saw him at the Opera Ball when I was 17—as though he knew all my secrets. There were a few more now.

"I'm working on something called *The Bride*."

"Not a portrait of a woman in a white gown."

"Not exactly. Anyway, suddenly I wanted an evening with you."

"I think an evening with me can be arranged. I show special mercy to aging painters."

He held my face between his hands and kissed me. His head bumped the green-shaded light hanging over the cutting table. It swung back and forth, causing abstract shadows to leap against the wall. "I like the mood you're in," I whispered.

The evening was perfect. The food was simple but delicious, the wine was heady and plentiful. We laughed, we teased, we acted very… young. Finally, we were the only couple left. The waiters slammed doors and sat by tables next to the kitchen, talking in dialect. By the time we strolled out into the night, we were warm and relaxed and our souls were flushed with contentment. It was the best time we'd had since Vali died.

Halos clung to street lights and snow floated like tiny pieces of embroidery all around us. I linked my arm lightly through his as we shuffled through the soft white night. Carriages and taxis slowed down, but we waved them on.

"We do many things well together. Walking is just one of them," Klimt said, biting my fingers through my gloves.

I stopped us under a streetlight, and fell in love with the creased face for the thousandth time. "Stay with me tonight. We haven't been together in a long time."

He tugged the collar of my cape around my throat. "Your patience over the years amazes me, Emilie."

"Me, too."

At my flat, we stood between the thick white draperies and the window pane, looking out on the gentle world of white, isolated from all past agony, from all future decisions. We melted into the waltz of a million snowflakes, into one another's familiar curves, into the rare floating state of oneness where thought slips away, and what you want is precisely what he wants at precisely the same moment.

And then the approaching roar, the waves of red dynamite behind my eyelids, my body... splintering into pinpricks of light in the dark... and now my skin is too new, too reborn to touch. I am a glittering part of a secret landscape of deep silent snow. Klimt strokes my hair, leading me into sleep.

At two o'clock, I opened my eyes and saw Klimt standing naked at the window, silhouetted against light from the street, his outline blurred by the soft hair that covered his body. I raised myself onto one elbow. "What?"

"I need to go. I'm restless." I watched him dress. The smock, the long cape, the fur hat to cover the balding head that looked sunburned even in the middle of the night in the middle of January.

"Thank you for tonight," I said.

"If anything, I should thank you, my friend." He pulled the covers up to my chin. "I think this will be a good year for us," he said gently. At the doorway, he turned. "Emilie?"

"Yes?"

"Nothing. I'll call you later in the week."

I lay staring at the rectangle of light. Snow drifted hypnotically outside the window. My heart was full.

,⁻.

18 January, 1918

At eight o'clock that morning, the phone rang. It was Consuela, Klimt's maid.

"Fraulein, he's just lying there! He can't move! What'll I do? He's just lying on the floor! All he said was, 'Call Emilie.'"

"Consuela, cover him with a blanket. Don't move him. Then call Dr. Bauer immediately. The number is right by the phone. Stop crying. You've got to be brave. I'll be there as soon as I can. Do you remember what I've told you?"

"I think so. Oh, I'm scared!"

"Go back and tell Herr Klimt that I'm coming and that Dr. Bauer is coming. After you've called the doctor, don't leave him, do you understand?"

"Ohhhhh!" she wailed.

"DO IT, CONSUELA!"

I don't remember dressing. I don't remember getting to Hietzing. I was numb. Consuela said Klimt had been taken to the Allgemeines Krankenhaus.

When I walked into his room, they'd already shaved off his beard. The strongest, most outrageous man I'd ever known laid there, a totally defenseless stranger. In the 27 years we'd been together, I'd never seen him without a beard, and it wasn't him.

Dr. Bauer and several nurses were doing things to him. He shook his head and frowned. "He wants these women to leave. He will not want anyone to take care of him. He will not want *me* to take care of him." I looked into Gustav's terrified eyes. "I will not leave you. We will not argue about this."

He closed his eyes and I felt a deadly pressure on my chest. I knew I would be living with this heavy ache for a long, long time. "I should be accustomed to this feeling by now," I thought. "I'm not."

Over the next two weeks I bathed him, fed him, read to him, and monitored the length of time each visitor spent with him. I forbade most people to see him. I tried to comfort Heli and his sisters. Georg found it especially hard.

Klimt's room resembled a funeral parlor. Alma Schindler Mahler Almost-Kokoschka Gropius not-quite-Werfel sent a bouquet every day for a week. The accompanying perfumed notes were the librettos for grand opera.

Monday: *"A little piece of my bright youth died when I learned that you were ill!"*

Tuesday: *"I would rush to your side but I'm afraid A Certain Person would do me grave physical harm!"*

Wednesday: *"We have looked for one another always in other people and not found each other!"*

Thursday: *"The name Gropius lies like barbed wire against my skin. I will be Mahler throughout eternity. I might have been Klimt if Fate had allowed!"*

Friday: *"You must get well and paint me while I am still beautiful! Kokoschka never did me justice!"*

Klimt managed a crooked smile. With great effort, he said, "Alma has strong hands from applauding her reflection in the mirror every day."

I was overjoyed. It was the most he'd said since the stroke. I sought encouragement from Dr. Bauer. "If he can talk, he'll be able to… do other things, it's just a matter of time, right?"

Dr. Bauer was cautious. "He's gaining more control over his speech, yes, but he's running a fever and he's coughing. He's still a very sick man. I don't think you should be here, Emilie. You're exhausted. You won't do him any good if you're ill, too. Besides, there's some influenza going around."

"Go home," Klimt said weakly. "'We're not going to argue about this.' That's a famous quote. Name escapes me."

.⁻.⁻.⁻.⁻.⁻.⁻.⁻.⁻.⁻.⁻.⁻.⁻.⁻.⁻.⁻.⁻.⁻.⁻.

Vows

Rosi drew me a bath and Heli brought dinner on a tray. We barely spoke. Heli returned to my room later, and stood in the doorway, holding tightly to the doorknob.

"Aunt Emilie, would you like me to brush your hair?"

"Oh, Heli, that would be wonderful."

She picked up the brush from the dresser—the brush Klimt commissioned Hoffmann to make for me a lifetime ago.

"Aunt Emilie, is he going to die?"

"Heli, Heli, come here, let me hold you." I held her and thought about the evening I'd held her mother before Heli was born, right after Ernst died. And how Klimt had held me in this same bed when Vali died.

Loved ones leave, one way or another. The question is: How to give oneself completely, ardently, without hesitation, knowing that the most suffocating, strangling pain probably awaits. I believe the answer is: By being a whole human being in your own right, so that when someone you love leaves, you still have someone you love: Yourself. That's my noble theory. My other theory is to rage at the heavens if it makes you feel better.

"You love your Uncle Gustav very much, don't you Heli?"

"Oh, more than anyone. As much as Mother, I think."

"So do I. Well, if he dies, Heli, I think there is only one thing we can do. I think we need to incorporate everything he was that is dear to us into our own lives: His integrity, his humor, his enthusiasm for life, his willingness to take risks, his delight in the simplest things—stroking a kitten, planting flowers, eating breakfast. We will need to live every day in such a way that it will give him and us pleasure and satisfaction and pride."

Heli lifted her head from my breast and frowned. "Do you think you can do that?"

"I don't know, darling. I intend to try. I feel Pauline and Vali are now part of me. Of course, if he lives, he'll be as maddening as ever."

Heli smiled. "There's only one of him, isn't there?"

"Ohhh, yes, my sweet, only one."

The next morning when I arrived at the hospital, I met Otto Wagner on the steps. He looked old.

"Emilie, it should be me, not him. He is the greatest painter of them all, you know. I've always said that. I told Louise just yesterday—" He stopped and busied himself with pulling on his gloves. Louise Wagner died three years ago. He writes to her every day in his journal.

Wagner shook his august head. "You know, Klimt said this grand thing to me once. He said, 'They won't let me paint the pictures in the buildings they won't let you build.' Isn't that like him?"

"It certainly is, Otto. Thank you for coming."

He nodded, his eyes searching my face for consolation but there was nothing I could say to diminish his loss or mine. He patted my hand and walked slowly down the stairs, his breath puffing small clouds into the winter air.

A nurse rustled out of Klimt's room. "That man is back—the one with the eyes. He won't leave," she said grimly.

"It's all right. That man is his son," I told her.

Egon Schiele sat by the bedside, stroking the starched sheets with long, nervous fingers. The curtains were drawn but soft golden light illuminated the room. Schiele had kept vigil all night. He looked up at me and whispered furiously, "Goddamn it, Emilie, he'll be all right. He's strong as an ox."

"Strong as a bull," Klimt said, the left side of his mouth curving into a smile.

Schiele exploded in a sob of laughter. "Tomorrow I'll bring charcoal. I'll teach you how to draw with your left hand. It'll be a whole new career. I'll turn you into another Kokoschka."

"And have Loos and Kraus drooling over me? Don't think so." Klimt's voice was almost inaudible.

Schiele stood, looking much younger than his 28 years. He turned to me, his eyes helpless. "I love him, Emilie."

"Go paint," Klimt rasped. Schiele embraced me. It was the embrace of a child, not the libidinous Egon Schiele of Neulengbach..

After Schiele left, I stood at the foot of the bed, memorizing his face. He looked… happy. The sensual mouth, which was never this naked with the beard, looked soft and his face was relaxed, no longer drawn.

I sat next to the bed and massaged the quiet right hand. I didn't know if he were awake or not. After a while, he said quietly, "Emilie?"

"Yes, my darling."

"I think we should be married."

I sat there for at least a minute, I think.

"Emilie? Did you hear me? Don't make me repeat myself."

"Gustav… why, after all this time?"

"Because I think we finally know each other well enough." He opened his eyes. He looked merry!

"Are you sure?"

"Emilie, I'm a patient man."

"I'm sorry, it's just that this comes as somewhat of a surprise."

"You mean you haven't considered it before?"

"Don't make me angry, Gustav."

"Alright. So before I lose my patience and you lose your composure, I think we should be married."

"Oh, my dearest, as soon as you're better, we'll—"

"No, Emilie. Now. I mean now. Right here. Right now."

"My God, Gustav, you are still the most outrageous man I've ever known!"

"I should hope so." His smile, so lopsided, looked wicked. I loved it. Here I was, the best designer in Vienna with 80 seamstresses at my disposal, 400 friends and relatives who'd waited two decades to see this day, and here I was, being married in a hospital with only Alma's bouquets as witness. It wouldn't be legal, no one would ever know, most people wouldn't believe it anyway. But I understood. Marriage *Klimt* style.

"Are you ready, Fraulein Flöge?"

"I have been ready for 27 years, Herr Klimt."

He lay silent a moment. I could feel him gathering his strength. "You, Emilie Flöge, have been my guide, my helpmate, my counselor and my best friend. I trust you, I respect you, I depend upon you."

He read the question in my eyes. "Of course I love you. You are my eternal love. From this moment on, you are my wife, by beloved wife." He drew my hand to his lips.

"You, Gustav Klimt, have been the fullest, richest part of my life. I discovered passion through you. I learned devotion beyond passion through you. Our friendship will outlast all temporal pain…. I can't think what else to say."

"For once."

"Hush! By the love in our hearts, we are now husband and wife. I think we should say 'amen.'"

"I think we should say, To Every Age its Art, to Art its Freedom." I leaned over and kissed him. Even now, his mouth thrilled me. He closed his eyes.

"Rest," I said.

"The light… in this room… is fascinating. I must do something about that, Frau Klimt."

"Yes, my darling. You will."

I stood beside the bed, stroking his forehead, the deep furrows above the eyebrows, the untamed hair at the temples. At some point, he slipped seamlessly into a coma. Then the doctors took over and I was pulled into a blur.

Klimt's sisters and Georg and dear Heli came each day. And every artist in Vienna came, even though Dr. Bauer no longer allowed visitors. They brought flowers and stood about in the waiting room, just to be close to him.

Karl Kraus came! He'd always hated Klimt's work. He chose his words carefully, as always. "Your friend has made my life more interesting. And, in an entirely different sense, you've made his life more interesting." He pursed his lips, bowed slightly and withdrew. I was touched.

The next afternoon I was pacing in the hospital garden when I saw a man who took my breath away. "You must be Gustav Klimt's son," I said.

"Yes. And you?"

"Emilie Flöge."

"Oh, of course. I've come to see him. Can you arrange it?"

"I'm sure I can. He's not conscious, you know."

"I just want to see him."

I led the young man into the hospital. He looked exactly like the Klimt I knew so many years ago—the same broad body, receding hairline, contentious beard and eyes that could bore through brick walls. The duty nurse recognized him, too. Her mouth and eyes made a perfect trio of matching O's.

I looked at this stranger with the face I knew so well. "Which one are you?" I asked.

"Gustav Ucicky. You've been through a lot, I expect."

I smiled.

"Did you hate him sometimes?" the young Gustav asked.

"Oh, absolutely."

"You're not a saint then. I was afraid you'd be a saint."

"Can you really imagine Gustav Klimt consorting with saints?"

The young man spent several days, sitting by the bedside, staring at his father.

One evening, Kolo and Ditha Moser marched into the hospital and announced, "We are kidnapping you for dinner." Kolo always made me feel good. Being in their home helped me believe that, yes, there was life outside the ivory walls of a hospital. I needed to tell him my secret.

"Gustav married me, Kolo. In his room, last week."

"He has always been married to you, Emilie, in his way," Kolo said gently, reaching across the table to cover my hand with his.

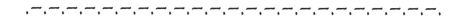

The Last Smock

On 6 February, 1918, Gustav Klimt died. I did what I knew how to do: I went to the shop and built him a new smock. I used a rich, tender wool, full and luxurious and sensual to the touch. It was the color of the Attersee in August. I worked all night.

In the morning, I wrapped it in brown paper and took it to Dr. Bauer. Klimt could not bear the thought of an open casket. He had told Georg, "Tell them to look at my paintings, don't let them look at me." I knew he would rather stride into eternity wearing a smock than a hated stuffy suit.

Many people were still at the hospital. Schiele drew a final portrait. A death mask was made. My… husband looked serene.

Schiele followed me into the hospital corridor. "Emilie?" He pushed his thick, tousled hair back from his forehead. "You smell good, Emilie. I know you loved Vali and I can only guess how much Klimt meant to you. I loved them, too, you know. I intend to make them both proud of me. Next month, I have a one-man show at the good old Secession. Klimt loved the irony of that."

He looked over my shoulder—seeing a memory that colored his cheeks. "About Vali—I still don't understand why she wouldn't share me. I didn't love her any less just because I married someone else. But paintings and drawings of her will be in the Secession show. I'll be famous one day, Emilie—and then, so will she. Let me take you home."

"No, I need to walk. But thank you, Egon. You've been a good… son."

As soon as I stepped into the dazzling winter sunshine—so rare for Vienna in February—I knew: Klimt had indeed done something about the light.

And I knew something else, Heli. Your Father, my Father, Pauline, Vali—they have not left us. And Gustav Klimt will not leave us either.

He is… in… this… air… right now….

END NOTES

The Swestern Flöge on Mariahilferstrasse closed in 1938, following the Anschluss. (In the late 1980's, I talked my way into the former fashion salon's space, located over a shoe store on the ground floor, so that I could look out the windows to see what Emilie saw. The company that occupied the space had never heard of Emilie Flöge.) During the Second World War, Emilie lived in a handsome house on the Attersee, which I've visited, far away from the destruction taking place in Vienna that began in earnest with the first Allied bombing 12 April, 1945. Following the war, Emilie resided in Vienna at Ungarsgasse 39, where she maintained a locked "Klimt room" containing many of his possessions: Japanese objets' art, drawings, hundreds of postcards, etc. A photograph taken by Viennese friend Florian Decker shows me standing in front of the building's massive wooden front door. (The 28 journals detailing my trips to Vienna are close-to-my-heart souvenirs of my love affair with the City of Dreams, and one of its most fabled residents.) Emilie died in 1952 at age 77. I have already outlived her by many years. If there is a Great Get Together In The Sky (or wherever), I expect we will share Klimt, one way or another....

ACKNOWLEDGEMENTS

To my late friend Professor Christian Nebehay, who gave me his gracious friendship, his expert guidance, and his vast knowledge of Klimt (whom he met when he was eight; Klimt had called upon Christian's father and played with little Christian, who told me the great painter was "very nice to me.")... To Reneé Nebehay, who welcomed me many summers into their lovely country home in Pulkau where, in return, I was assigned to harvest whatever was ripe in their orchards ... To my lovely and lively "grandmother" Dr. Vita Kunstler, who always wanted to walk rather than take public transportation so that she could show me "hidden Vienna"; she was in her 90s at the time; I cherish memories of tea in Vita's study under and gaze of Klimt's painting of *Amelia Zuckerkandl*, now gracing a wall at the Belvedere; I promised Vita that after she died, I would set up a table in the museum in front of Amelia and have tea, but I only managed a cheese sandwich... To America's Ambassador to Austria in the late 1980s, Ronald Lauder, who was so helpful to me when I lost my passport; prior to my first trip to Vienna in May 1987, we'd shared correspondence centering on our mutual appreciation of Klimt and Schiele; after returning to America, Lauder founded the elegant Neue Gallery in NYC... To the late Ruth Brinkmann, Co-Artistic Director of Vienna's English Theater (VET), who offered me, during a late night supper with the persuasive Nebehays, the opportunity to stage *Vienna Patterns* at VET ... To Nicholas Allen, the charming British/Austrian director of VET's wonderful touring school programs, my conduit to VET and Forever Friend... To the cast of VET's staged reading of *Vienna Patterns* with Austria's best-known American composer, the late and dearly missed Eugene Hartzell; beautiful British actress Melinda May, who was the perfect Alma Mahler and the late Michael Peer, who was more Adolf Loos on VET's stage than Loos was at the Café Museum... To Paul van der Lubbe, VET's Technical Director, who provided all a writer/director could want as support to the *Vienna Patterns* production; Paul is also a Forever Friend who takes me to theater openings in Vienna and horse races in Bratislava ... To Michael Marinucci, Director of Theater at the American International School in Vienna, who arranged the 1989 *Vienna Patterns* auditions at a Tex-Mex restaurant run by a gay black man from Culpeper, VA; Michael and I have worked and played together ever since ... To Cynthia Reitter, VET's retired Box Office Manager and my political soulmate; we solve the problems of the world during my annual visits ... To Jennifer Muellner and the Hotel Bleckmann staff, who make me feel that Vienna is indeed my true home ... To my close friend, the late Dr. Meredith Rode, artist and brilliant woman, who called *Vienna Patterns* "delicious." (She told a class, "A sunset in Yosemite National Park is awesome. The color of nail polish is not." Brava!) To another marvelous friend, psychotherapist and balletomane Jona Clarke, who knew everything that was worth knowing ... To Dr. Felicity Scheier and Georg Becker, who served as founders and past presidents of The Gustav Klimt Memorial Society (I am a charter member); they were responsible for keeping Klimt's last atelier from the clutches of those who would not grant the building the care and respect it deserves ... To Dr. Salomon Grimberg, art history detective, who rendezvoused with me for an hour in the Dallas Airport so that we might meet in person after many telephone conversations about Klimt... To Salomé Gongadze and Santiago Mallan, my charming and indispensable teenage interns, who helped me become wary friends with my mysterious computer... To an irresistible taskmaster, Frank J. Mendelson, who encouraged me to publish after I'd stopped trying... Finally, I extend profound appreciation to my family and friends who, over the years, have listened to me grumble and rhapsodize about my love affair with Klimt ... And if you notice tiny pieces of paper floating in the air, it's celebratory confetti tossed at the agent who rejected this manuscript with the snarl, "No one's ever heard of Gustav Klimt and no one's ever heard of you!" (Klimt enjoyed that comment. I didn't.)

ABOUT THE AUTHOR

JOAN KELLEY was born on a farm in Erie, Pennsylvania and began writing and illustrating her stories in a bales-of-hay house her father built for her in the barn. At Ohio Wesleyan University, Kelley majored in English and minored in theater and art. In the graduate program at the University of Wisconsin/Madison, she studied modern dance. Kelley has been a writer, modern dancer, actor, choreographer, producer/director, teacher, and for 25 years, a writer for federally supported programs such as The Peace Corps and VISTA. She is a Helen Hayes nominee and, not incidentally, the mother of six, grandmother of eleven, and great-grandmother of four.

Kelley has made 28 extended trips to Vienna since 1987, and has directed nine shows there — in the hometown if her heart. After fifty years in Arlington, Virginia, she now resides in Savannah, Georgia.

Made in the USA
Middletown, DE
10 March 2019